CW00405743

THE DEAD

&

THE DROWNING

A WHITE KNUCKLE ADVENTURE WITH A DARK HEART

CAMERON BELL

Cameron Bell

The characters and events portrayed in this book are fictitious. Any similarity to real persons, living or dead, is coincidental and not intended by the author. For the sake of authenticity some addresses, locales and organizations are real; however, any association with them, or representation of them are entirely fictitious.

Text copyright ©2019 Cameron Bell all rights reserved.

No part of this book may be reproduced, or stored in a retrieval system, or transmitted in any form or by any means, electronic, mechanical, photocopying, recording, or otherwise, without express written permission of the publisher.
Published 2019 Big Dune Books.

Cover Art Carl Greaves Extendedimagery.com

A big thank you to those that encouraged and helped me, you know who you are.

CHAPTER 1

9:07 pm Friday November 4[th,] 2017

Leaning against the bar I drain a fourth pint of Gull and feel like another. Booze always demanded more booze, and after a taste I am usually off to a decent swig. Drinking in downtown Reykjavik however, is not for the frugal or broke, and I had taken to a remedy. I had enjoyed an ample glass of the good stuff before leaving the hotel, then slammed the happy hour at the Gaukurinn. Tonight, it isn't enough, and having a mixture of feelings I can't settle - I drink on.

There is a music festival in the city and a three-piece indie band in ripped black clothing are on the stage playing hard and heavy. I had liked that type of music when I was young, music that drove you on, and over the years my taste had not really changed. They play to a throbbing crowd under a pitched roof of strobing red and blue lights; that flash me back to an earlier time of carefree gigs.

I work slowly on my beer and fight against a creeping melancholy that has dogged me for days. I had long wanted to travel to Iceland, albeit not like this - not on my own. We were meant to go together but kept putting it on the back burner for the sake of home improvements and child-friendly holidays. When it had been our time it had been too late. She suffered a massive dead on the spot stroke. It was as sudden and violent as a blindside collision. It left me reeling in grief and I have yet to find my feet.

My experience of grief is that it is a desolate, withering place where good feelings shrivel like a slug in the midday sun. I have stayed here too long my outlook has darkened. I have stripped life down to its cruel element: to one without god, without karma, without justice, to one that spat in your face when you dared to have plans. I subtly shake my head, and my body heaves a subdued and sickened laugh at it all.

My awful reverie is broken by a woman smiling at me. There had been a healthy gap between me and the next guy, who is hunched over the bar immersed in his phone; now with my broadness, it is tight and touching. She has Kronas in her hand so wants to be served, but she is looking at me – not the best way to get a drink I muse.

"They're not bad, are they?" she says cocking her head in the band's direction.

American, Canadian perhaps?

"Yes … remind me a little of *The Strokes*."

She smiled again, a wide attractive smile, crooked at the right showing uniform white teeth. I straighten up from a slouch, and she is just a smidge shorter than my five feet nine.

"I like your accent … is it Welsh?"

I return a little closed lip smile and reply,

"Yes, it is … I don't think most people outside of the UK would have got that."

"I suppose I'm not most people," is her answer.

This could have come off cocky, but a depreciating flick of her eyebrows told me she isn't full of herself. She stops smiling and looks over her shoulder.

"Now I'll show my ignorance and admit that I can't say whether you are American or Canadian."

"I'm from New Zealand," she replies straight-faced.

I screw my face quizzically.

"No, just messing with you … I'm from Buffalo in New York State … so really not that far from being Canadian." She laughs and sweeps her hand through thick, collar length black hair, that has a section buzz cut on the right side above the ear.

"Yes, I know of it, the Buffalo Bills Football Team yeah … and you used to have a prominent Mafia Family," I say awkwardly

4

not really thinking about what I was saying.

She pauses for a moment presumably to edit the nonsense I had just spouted and then carries on.

"You like football? I grew up watching the Bills with my dad and I try to catch all their games."

"I follow *The NFL Show*, and If I am able to I'll stay up and watch the Super Bowl."

"Do you want a beer? it's all right I'm an heiress and can afford it."

I find myself smiling, enjoying the diversion but then a wave of guilt washes over it. Is this harmless holiday chit-chat or is it leading to something? because at nine quid a throw buying a beer for someone meant something here.

"No, keep hold of your fortune I'm calling it a night," I reply meekly.

Without any effort, she catches the bartender's attention and calls for two Gulls.

"You wouldn't let a girl drink on her own, would you?"

The smile coquettish, powerful, like a hot dryer blasting ice – this woman has confidence.

"No, the gentleman in me couldn't allow such a terrible thing," I say with fake gallantry.

She hands me a beer and I glimpse part of a tattoo peeking out of the right sleeve of her jacket. I can't make out what it is, but it isn't a small cutesy design. The colours are bold against the paleness of her inner forearm and I imagine it stretches back to her elbow.

I neck the remainder of my beer and make a start on the one just bought. I am now well lubricated and a couple or so more would see me drunk. Her eyes did a fast sweep of the bar and then return to me.

"So! doing the tourist thing or are you here for work?" I ask.

"Vacation ... booked a couple of hotels, hopped on a plane, hired a car ... and just explored. How about you?"

"Needed to get away, though pretty much the same except for the car. I like organized adventure."

She laughs,
"Isn't that a kind of an oxymoron like virtually spotless?"
"It is," I agreed, smiling freely.
"I'm William by the way."
"Toni with an I."
We talk, and the beer goes down.

"One for the road," I exclaim in a theatrical voice, the Kronas out and waving. I get my round in and blank out what it costs.
"Where are you staying?" she asks.
"The Storm Hotel."
"I'm near there; you can be a gentleman and walk me some of the way," she suggests persuasively.
She didn't strike me the type that wanted looking after, and I didn't feel ready for anything else, but walking her back to her hotel couldn't do any harm.
"Yes, Ma'am."

We talk some more, and I learn that she is a tattoo artist and owns her own parlour in a small city outside of Buffalo. She then politely asks me what I do, and not wanting to talk about it I lie.

We step outside, and Toni looks behind her towards the door.
"Is something wrong?"
"No ... no, nothing," nonchalant, but not quite.
She seemed alternatively uber together and a little skittish, a peculiar blend that has me intrigued. I decide to let it lie, denying a habit of sniffing around for dirt in the dark corners of people's lives - no, not tonight.

The night air is crisp and sobering, the moon an opaque disc behind the clouds. It is a Friday night in early November, and it is strange as a Brit not to see or hear fireworks. We head up onto Laugavegur: clots of revellers hunch against the cold smoking cigarettes between bars, while coaches clog the streets picking up tourists to see the Northern Lights. The city is lively but not as busy as the few other capitals I had visited; it is instead quirky and charming, and I find myself liking it.

We get close to my hotel.

"Well, I'm almost home, where are you?"

"Here will do," she said looking down a long, narrow cut through between two tall, grey buildings.

I am a bit drunk and my tongue is loose and careless.

"Well it has been a treat meeting you Toni, perhaps our paths will cross again ... in a bar in Iceland."

Toni broke that wide grin and replied,

"Who knows ... maybe, never, certain."

A good line to depart on I thought and walk on.

I had taken a few steps when I remember that I hadn't phoned my daughter like I was supposed to. I fish out my phone and then pat around my clothing for my glasses. It isn't too late to phone, though having said that I am too pissed to speak to someone who is probably sober, so a short text would be better. I am in on the contact when I hear a shout, and then a shriek, a pause then a scream. The phone goes back in the pocket and I run back to the cut through.

She is on her back with one man clamping her legs, and another crouching over her head fighting her arms - she is wriggling like a mad woman and turning the air blue.

"Hand it over!" I hear one of them demand.

"Go fuck yourself!" is her fiery reply.

It never pays to announce yourself, so I don't. I dash forward and cover the yards, stuttering my stride like a bowler for the last few, and blast the crouching fella behind the ear with a cheap shot right cross that reverberates up my arm. He drops like a slaughterhouse cow and lays crumpled in an untidy, motionless heap.

I reset and turn on the other guy. He springs to his feet and a right and left I have planned for him swipe air as he adeptly slips back and slides right. On his toes bouncing, wide stance, left arm out, right hand at the waist – a Karate fighter. He is rangy and bad boy handsome with short, harsh bottle blonde hair, and a large throat tattoo. He is in his mid to late thirties, around six

feet tall, a slender V-shape with slim legs in tight-fit jeans. He shrugs the dark, shiny ribbed jacket he is wearing and beckons me with his lead hand. In a gravelly voice, he says,
"Come on let's dance."

I almost laugh at the cheesy bravado and unimpressed I charge, but I am stopped in my tracks with a stabbing front kick to the guts. I double over and fight against spewing and dropping to the ground. I straighten up and I am met with a blitzing attack of straight punches. I duck and crab up in a cross-guard shell and weave. A punch scuffs along my scalp and the others are blocked and slipped.

Then from low I whip upward from my socks a leaping left hook that Joe Frazier would have been proud of. He anticipates and pulls back, but not enough, and my fist wallops the point of his jaw violently tilting his head to turn him off. His ass hits the concrete and the force ripples through his upper body leaving him straining upwards, glassy-eyed and out of it. I am admiring my handiwork when Toni stomps him in the head and makes him go limp.

There is a lot to say but not here. I grab her arm and command,
"Come with me!"
She does, and we run out into the street and around the corner to The Storm. Inside I acknowledge the greeting of the receptionist and open the fire door to access the stairway. My room is on the second floor. I get the key card out ready and in we go.
I turn to Toni,
"You okay?"
"I think so … I mean yeah … thank you for jumping in like that."
"It was the right thing to do, so I did it," I said as plainly as I could.
She appeared a little shaken, though less than you would expect.
"Still, you could have got hurt … thanks."
I give a settling smile,
"Well thankfully on this occasion it's the scumbags left with the sore heads."

"Yeah, you really gave it to them."

"I've had some practice."

She is about to say something else, but I cut across her,

"Well, do you mind telling me what happened there?"

"What do you mean?"

"I mean why did those two men attack you?"

"I don't know ... rape, robbery ... why do men attack women?" she replies in narky tone.

"I don't buy it, this is Reykjavik, not Mexico City; I think you were expecting trouble."

A bad play made too soon, tact had taken a back seat, and bluntness is drunk at the wheel.

"I don't need this right now ... I think I ought to go to the police."

Toni takes a short step to the door, though keeps her eyes on me – if I had a barcode, she would be reading it.

"Let's keep them out of it."

"Why?"

It was my turn to feel on the spot.

"Because I don't need the hassle ... I'm here to blow off some steam, see some sights ... and the police station isn't one of them."

She goes to the door and grips the handle, pauses, and then releases it. She looks at me, or more accurately she scrutinizes me like I am an unknown factor in an equation.

"Okay ... cards on the table. The second guy you flattened, he is my Ex. Marcus. We split up a few weeks ago ... and he is ... a completely vile, jealous, possessive asshole. I saw him earlier in another bar ... wasn't sure if he saw me or not ... though he must have."

Toni finishes with her palms open like a magician performing a trick.

"And you picked me to be your guard dog?"

"Yes, though you are marginally better looking than a guard dog." She expresses this with a smirk and a shrug of the eyebrows, and it lessens the sting.

"Charming," I say in mock offense.

"Well! if it nurses your fragile male ego, I chose you because you are pretty solid looking, you know big back and shoulders, head like a bucket, good for graft as my grandmother would say."

Toni spreads her hands, and with an expression of appreciation pretends to hold something substantial and meaty.

Chuckling, I put my palms up in surrender,

"All right all right, I think I prefer being compared to a guard dog. Okay, so who then is the other bloke ... I mean guy?"

"Adam Kucera, Marcus's cousin; they grew up in each other's pockets. If Marcus had ever killed me and there were times when he came close, Adam would have gladly helped him dig the hole."

"Touching."

"He's a real piece of work, done time for hanging a dog."

"Hanging a dog," I echo.

"Yeah, when he was eighteen he hung his neighbour's dog from a tree because the dude told him to stop parking in front of his driveway."

I point to her and say with amusement,

"He's what you call a douche bag right?"

"You know your American insults."

"I like American crime movies: *Goodfellas, Carlito's Way, Heat.* I sometimes think I know as much about American culture as my own."

   My part had been explained, and at this point I didn't need to know any more, though I suspected there was a lot more to it all than she was letting on. The men wanted something she has, and she doesn't want to tell me what that is. Toni is trouble, and in my room; the wise move is to cut her loose and carry on with the sight-seeing. But the juices are flowing, and the heartbeat drums a dangerous rhythm – I want to play.

"You used me, and I'm fine with that. You needed to do what you needed to do," I state sympathetically.

"That's cool of you to say that."

Her mind whirs for a few seconds, her tongue coiled against her teeth.

"Would you help me again?"

"I might, but I'm not digging any holes," I respond with a grin.

"I'll save that for our second date," she quips back.

 I'm getting to like this woman, she's as sharp as a cut-throat razor.

CHAPTER 2

09:11am Wednesday March 29[th,] 2017.

  I saw the call before it was put out over the air. I had emptied the sector inbox for the second time that morning and switched applications to check on the live incidents. It appeared on the screen in red, which meant it was still being processed – a sudden death. I clicked on it and read the text: a man had been found hanging from a tree on a hillside overlooking Blaencwm - a little dead-end village off the main-line of the Rhondda Fawr Valley. I would be required to go, but first I needed to allocate a unit to attend. I checked availability, Foxtrot Echo 44 and 46 were free. I went over the air and asked the control room to attach them to the call, and to also inform the Bronze Inspector. I attached myself to the incident, picked up the Kuga keys off the board and left the office.

  It was off the beaten track; a B road led to a country lane, which turned into a pitted track and ended at a farm. Not being in the division that long I had gone off course, and had to be guided in by the sat nav. I left the Kuga in the farmyard, negotiated a gate and crossed a dewy field on foot. Thankfully the ground was firm, and the field was full of sheep and not cows. I kept my eyes low to avoid the copious amounts of sheep shit, and the boots got wet and not filthy. I reached the end and scaled another gate, my weight heavy on the fall, cuffs clattering on the belt, slight twinge in my ankle – age did not come alone.

  The field sloped downwards towards the bottom of the valley

and had a solitary tree a middle of the way across, and a quarter of the way down. The tree was old with overhanging branches and exposed roots. I could see Mike standing at the side of it smoking an e-cigarette, and Sarah alongside the trunk of the tree using a job Samsung. I ambled down.

"All right Mike, Sarah?"

"Yeah ... found us eventually then," Mike cracked.

"I took the scenic route."

Mike Francis fizzed with nervous energy and if he wasn't fidgeting or talking your ears off, he was vaping. He was thin to the point of needing a good feed, but whatever he ate he burned off. Prior to joining the police he'd been a carpenter and still was, taking cash in hand jobs either side of his shifts. Like me Sarah was new to the team, she was a petite university graduate that wanted to get on the Public Protection Unit investigating sexual abuse cases.

I took a few more paces and saw a sad, scrawny figure sat slouched on his left leg like a puppet held up with only one string. The string was taut blue nylon rope pressing deep into the neck underneath the jaw. The rope created an ugly indent and kinked his head straight against the lean of his body. The tongue, a strangled purple leaked from the mouth and the eyes with a freckle of blood stared blankly ahead at the hillside. The rope from the branch to the neck was a short length. It had been wound several times around a sturdy branch, and the knot in the untidiness of his hair was thick and over tied – he had clearly meant to get it done.

"It is our Mis-per Sarge," said Sarah and she showed me on the Samsung a mugshot of Arthur Lewis.

He was a local man aged thirty-eight, and had been missing for forty hours, and by the rigor mortis that had set in had been dead for a good number of them. A petty criminal with a persistent drug problem, he had been in and out of prison and had lived off benefits his entire adult life. He had lived alone in a flat provided by a housing association and had been reported missing by his twenty year old daughter. Like many of the people I dealt with he was a sufferer of depression and anxiety and took a cocktail of meds and other substances to blot life out. Given the hand he had been dealt in life, and the despairing grind in flailing and falling, fucking up and failing; I understood how he had arrived here on the mountainside, put a noose around his neck, and just sat down. I was surprised more people didn't do the same.

I broke away from morbid thoughts and got the ball rolling; the deceased had been found just over an hour ago by a dog walker - they always found people. The dog walker was sitting in her car in a lay-by on the other side of the field. Mike had taken an account from her and had asked her to stay until I came. I read the account, it was comprehensive, and she didn't need to stay. The scene was easy to manage it was established, with no blood or other evidential material and free of people.

The next thing to do was to work through the list of professionals that would need to attend. Mike had already called for the paramedics so that death could officially be pronounced. I went over the air and rattled the others off requesting: C.I.D. Crime Scene Investigation, and the Force Medical Examiner; I would leave the undertaker until last.

The paramedics were first to arrive to perform a perfunctory role. They hooked up an E.C.G. on his lifeless body and the machine told everyone what they already knew. A form was filled out, and Sarah got the yellow copy to staple to the F13 death form submitted to the Coroner, giving a time that life was pronounced extinct. C.I.D. and C.S.I. arrived together. The young Detective Nathan Keller didn't have much to offer and clearly didn't want to be there. He kept looking at his shiny, office shoes and was complaining about a complex case file he needed to get back to. I told him that I had it covered and that I would update him if the Doctor had a Columbo moment and cried foul play. Stumpy the CSI was an old sweat, thirty years as a Copper and a further seven after retirement as a civilian CSI. We caught up as he took photographs and measurements.

We got lucky with the Doc, who was just leaving Merthyr

Tydfil when he got the call. A quarter of an hour after the others, Doctor Kozek, a heavyset Pole with a stomach like a barrel, waddled tentatively down the field. His corpulence making him ill-suited to even a short spell rambling over uneven ground. He reached us in a state of discomfort, and for a moment there was the black thought that we may have two deaths on our hands. The Doctor nodded a greeting and took a silent minute to settle the strain. Then when he was ready, he put a pair of latex gloves on and examined the body for trauma.

He checked the head, neck, chest, and back for ligature marks and wounds. He said to me,

"Can I have the body down please?"

Stumpy cut the rope midway to preserve the knot, and I lowered Lewis to the grass. Doctor Kozek then unbuttoned Lewis's trousers and inspected the left leg and buttock.

"Yes, see the blood pooling ... it is as it should be. He hang in this ... situation and the blood sink down to here."

I updated Bronze by phone that there were no suspicious circumstances and left Mike and Sarah arrange the undertakers.

I got back to the Kuga and fell into the seat. I had only managed to grab a few hours sleep and now I was struggling. Death now fatigued me, it didn't use to, and in such situations, I was closer to indifferent than compassionate. That had changed when my wife had died; it wasn't that it made me care more for the death of others, it was that their death amplified my own grief. It had been eighteen months, but it often felt like eighteen hours. I started the car and headed back along the valley towards the station in Ton Pentre.

CHAPTER 3

I was driving out of Treorchy when the Control Room put out a 999 call.

"Immediate response: Thirteen Margaret Street, Pentre. Female Jade Hanford reporting that her ex-partner Nicky Larkin is outside kicking the door in."

I racked my brain for where it was, the location vague in my mind. The call was put out again over the radio - I jumped in anyway,

"Foxtrot Echo 40 on route."

"Roger that, are you single crewed?"

"Yes, yes."

"I'll see if I can get another unit to back you up. Jade Hanford is a high-risk victim of domestic abuse from Nicky Larkin. Larkin has warning signals for weapons, violence, drugs, escaper, fail to appear, offends on bail. He also has a wanted marker ... his licence has been revoked and he has been recalled to prison."

Nicky Larkin - this was not going to go well. I had a history with Larkin; he was nothing special to me, just one of a number over the years that I had had regular run-ins with. However, he did not feel the same way; he thought I had it in for him and he hated the fuck out of me. I first had dealings with him when he burgled a school in Port Talbot at age fourteen, and our paths must have crossed at least a couple of dozen times in the proceeding eleven years. There had been foot pursuits, cycle chases, searches; there had been abuse, threats and fights, interviews and court cases. He had assaulted me, I had assaulted him, and he had made complaints against me which hadn't gone anywhere. He had bragged to other Port Talbot scrotes that he would run me over, and in the right circumstances he might have. In the right or wrong circumstances, he was capable of practically anything.

The last I heard he was over the wall doing a four year stretch for a knifepoint robbery of a betting shop - he needed double that to cool his heels and wear him down. Although, in reality he had probably only served just over two before being released on licence. Larkin, a Port Talbot boy was off patch, as was I - an old rivalry to be resumed on new ground.

I pulled in to the side of the road, got my smartphone out, opened Google maps and put the address in. It was the third left turn on the road I was on, and I was less than thirty seconds from it. No lights or sirens - it didn't pay to raise alarm and have him scoot.

I took the third left turn and climbed a steep street of old terraced housing that had been built for miners at the beginning of the last century. I dropped down a gear and crossed over the junction with Hill Side Street. Then I dumped the Kuga at a careless angle near the end of the street and got out to check for house numbers. Thirteen was on the left side of the road and end of the terrace; and it was the right address because the white UPVC front door was off the hinges.

I turned my radio down and entered cautiously from the pavement, pausing in the hallway to listen, the naked stairs in front of me, the lounge to the right. I heard a commotion from the back of the house; a burst of adrenaline felt like falling and my limbs shook. I stepped into the drab, sparsely furnished lounge with its nicked walls and battered sofa. A stale smell thick, heavy and ingrained clogged my nostrils and the stains on the cheap laminate floor stuck to the soles of my Altberg boots. I heard Larkin's crude voice from the enclosed kitchen behind,

"It's not fucking over ... it's not. I loves you Jade and I want us back together ... I can change, I have fucking changed for fuck's sake! Gimme another chance, c'mon!"

Larkin was pleading, but all the same there was bite in his

voice, and he wouldn't plead for long before he snapped and hit. How to play this? I spun through factors and options: kitchen meant pans and knives, confined space and Jade an unknown element in the crossfire. Reasoning with him would be pointless, CS spray was out - everyone would end up getting some and it affected me badly. I could go straight for the ASP, but if used this ran the risk of catching Jade on the backswing. Another problem was with a baton in hand I wouldn't be able to handcuff. Then it would be fast in and hands on; try to keep hold of the fucker and wait for the cavalry to arrive. I readied myself and crept along the separating wall towards the archway, my view of the kitchen limited to the side of the fridge.

"Get the fuck offa me! We've been through this a million times: rows, girls, drugs, police, prison ... it's doing my fucking head in. You turn up here, kick the fucking door in telling me you've changed. Yeah, big fucking change ... twat!" complained and provoked a female voice, harsh and caustic, running the gamut of tone and pitch.

"Are you fucking someone else, is that it, is that what you've been up to? I'm going to turn this shit-hole upside down, and if I find anything that proves you're fucking behind my back ... I'll fucking do you, I swear, I'll open your slut face like a fucking purse."

I moved into the archway and Larkin was standing with his back to the fridge – I was shocked at what I saw, and a queasy spill of adrenaline sank into my gut. Larkin had bulked up. No longer was he a stringy and Mephedrone gnawed lunatic bouncing around Sandfields Estate like a demented jack-in-the-box. He must have hit the weights hard in jail and probably the roids to; he was now a very solid six feet two head case entering his prime. He had five inches and twenty years on me, though probably in truth not that much weight.

I leapt at him nonetheless and clamped double grips on his left arm at the wrist and elbow. I tried to turn the elbow for an entangled arm lock and wasn't quick enough in the execution. Larkin instinctively stiffened his arm into a rigid pole, then jerked it back to pivot and turn into me,

"Cutter," he spat.

His hatchet like face flashed hateful malice, and I caught sight of his stubby, malnourished baby teeth. Greyed and ground down by stimulant drugs and bruxism. Larkin leant back and heaved, and I was pulled like a hooked fish. He was strong, so I went with it and crashed him into the back door. We grappled against the door, the UPVC giving to our weight. I sought to arrest, he to get away. I crowded him with my shoulders and pressed my forehead into his cheek, and intimate information was exchanged in our struggle: the stench of cigarettes, small cries and bad sweat. I could feel his desperation, and perhaps he could sense my fear, not of violence, but of the peril of restraint.

"Fuck you Cunter," he spat in rage.

Cunter was a name they had for me. I replied low and cold,

"We'll see who gets fucked."

Larkin grabbed a handful of hair with one hand and cupping the back of my head with the other yanked me bent. I strained to straighten up, but got nowhere, he had me locked down tight. There was a brief pause and I cross guarded my face; then I felt an upward smash and my skull shuddered. I caught another knee on my forearm, and a further cracked my forehead. The red mist descended, no more half measures, one of us would fall.

I could see waistline and down and there was only one spot to hit. I shifted position and banged away angrily with both fists - the release pleasurable. Rocking and bouncing around the grimy, chip pan kitchen, I hit hip and thigh and took a glancing blow along the jawline. I dug in a hard hook close to the payoff and could feel Larkin flinch, and then spasm into further violence, rag dolling me up to speed and launching me at the sink. I slammed shoulder first into the unit below, and not knowing if I was hurt or not, flipped over with my hands up anticipating a follow-up boot in the face. It didn't come; Larkin was at the back door.

I rolled to my feet and followed through the flung open door, along the cracked garden path, Larkin bounding ahead. The gate was blocked by an upturned sofa and bags of refuse, so Larkin veered right, through a knotted morass of grass and brambles and vaulted with abandon at the six-foot wall. The grass had hampered him, and Larkin had only got half over by the time I had reached the wall. Chest astride the top, with his left leg cocked over and the other dangling in front of me. I seized the dangling leg at the ankle and calf, and furiously with all my weight and strength cranked the leg outward against the knee. I pulled like an incensed dog, repeatedly wrenching the limb against its natural motion. Larkin howled, and the knee cricked and cracked, and the whole thing looked and sounded hideously comic. I then callously tossed him over the wall, and he cried out again.

I quickly heaved myself over the wall to see him already on his feet and hobbling down an alley towards the main road. I chased him down and caught up with him without effort. Larkin heard my heavy approach and stopped, turned and raised his hands.
"Fuck off!" raw, full of exasperation and anger; his brow split and bleeding he edged forward.
I answered from a distance with a spearing left jab to the kisser. Larkin's head whipped back, and wrong-footed he stumbled on his heels like a drunk Cossack, collapsing noisily against a blue metal garage door. He lay propped up awkwardly next to a smear of dog shit and pieces of broken glass. Larkin looked up at me. The pupils of his eyes dilated to black beads and his mouth bloodied. I stared down at him wanting to do more,
"Enough! ... you are under arrest for using violence to secure entry."
I drew my CS spray, Larkin looked beaten – I hosed him anyway and watched him crawl on his hands and knees amidst the glass and shit, spluttering mucus and snot, streaming tears, eyes screwed tight against the burning crystals. What they called me was undeserved, but not wholly undeserved.

Back-up arrived, and Larkin was cuffed and stuffed into the back of a police van and taken to Merthyr Custody. All the way up the Rhondda Fawr Valley he headbutted the cage and threatened to rape our wives and burn down our houses – this was not unusual, and it was water off a duck's back. Larkin kicked up a fuss at the custody desk complaining that his knee was fucked, which in fairness it probably was. I had some bumps and bruises, so arrested him for assault police. During the caution, I could barely conceal my enjoyment as he went off his nut in an indignant tantrum. We'd keep the recall to prison for later after the investigations into the offences were concluded.

The Custody Sergeant authorized Larkin's detention and directed that he be taken to the hospital. Larkin was escorted to the hospital by a couple of my team, checked out, patched up and brought back for an interview, charging and shipping off back to prison on the revocation of his licence.

Meanwhile, I spent three enjoyable hours writing a tactical statement, comprehensively rationalizing and justifying my actions. An old Sergeant of mine had once given me some sage advice. He told me that you must paint a picture, a vivid picture, so it can be seen that what you did in the circumstances was the only thing that you could have reasonably done. In this case some of it was a stretch, nevertheless with a little creative license I made it all fit.

CHAPTER 4

The fallout was brutal. I had expected a complaint and one was made. Removed from the chaotic mash of crisis and criminality Larkin had time to seethe, and stew and get even. The sickener was how hard they came at me. The Inspector handling the case had flown up the ranks and was on the fast track to becoming a Chief Inspector. He was doing a six-month attachment in the Professional Standards Department and he wanted a scalp for his portfolio.

Alexander Pritchard-Hayes was smart and repugnantly ambitious and wanted to demonstrate his integrity by throwing me under a bus. I had I suppose made myself a viable target, in that I had been in this position before, in fact, several times in twenty-three years policing at the sharp end of society. However, it was my belief that if you stood in harm's way, you often had to do harm yourself. I admired how Orwell had put it,

"People sleep peacefully in their beds at night only because rough men stand ready to do violence on their behalf."

Pritchard-Hayes served the Regulation fifteen on me and I was told that I was to be placed on restricted duties. This meant that I was to have no direct contact with the public. During our meeting I noticed that he had slate grey, reptilian eyes, and these were set in a smooth almost bust like face that watched you with the cold dispassion of a predator. I was an opportunity to be had and could expect no mercy - he was Caligula and I was getting the downward thumb. He treated me like a Pleb too. There was the guise of courtesy and respect, but it was thin, and it couldn't hide a superior conceit and a downward looking gaze. I nodded and said as little as possible even though I wanted to knock the smugness out of him. I was stoic and almost silent, lest give him any rope to hang me with.

I ran my eyes over his smart business suit, soft manicured hands and fifty quid haircut and I despaired. He was a breed of police that spent as little time as possible dealing with criminals, and as much of it as possible to further his career. Policing itself wasn't really important, he could have sold soup for what it mattered provided he reached top echelon of management. I disliked people like him – butterflies flitting around the organization trying to look pretty, attaching themselves to projects, creating mostly useless initiatives with sexy acronyms – they were never going to get a bar stool across the back of the head. Ah, but could these feelings be tainted by the bitterness of envy, and the inadequacy of stunted ambition – I didn't like to dwell on that, it was more comfortable being a self-righteous martyr of the front line.

So, I was relocated to the Criminal Justice Unit, a tedious back office job processing case files. I worked eight to four Monday to Friday with civilians, retired officers and serving officers too afraid to get their hands dirty, where the only risk of harm was neck strain and a paper cut – I despised it. All the times I had put myself on the line, the scrapes, the knocks, the grief counted for nothing. The Sergeant I replaced wanted to get back out and he slipped into my job like a favoured son – whilst I felt I had been tossed in a bin. The only upside was I had more opportunity to get out on the mountain with the rifle to hunt. Proper policing is similar in certain respects to hunting, and because I could no longer police I hunted more. My freezer was filled to the brim, and my father's whippet ate like a king.

After about six weeks I was invited to Queens Road Police Station in Bridgend for a recorded interview, and in a side office was booked into the custody suite as a voluntary attendee.

The complaint I was facing was of assaulting Larkin and causing him actual bodily harm. It was a criminal investigation and gross misconduct, which meant that there was double jeopardy – criminal proceedings and disciplinary proceedings where I could be dismissed. I had a Federation Rep with me, and the Inspector had a Detective Sergeant in tow.

I got grilled for three hours. The Inspector gunned for me, the DS I felt purposely gave me his B game. He had investigated rotten cops and I wasn't one of them, heavy handed maybe, rotten no, and the complainant was a first division shitbag with eighty-four convictions.

I stuck to my statement, expanding and reinforcing where necessary. Pritchard-Hayes was used to winning, and flickers of frustration appeared on his face when he couldn't nail me as he wanted. The truth of it was the case against me was weak. Hanford wouldn't get involved, there were no other witnesses, and I had not denied my actions so couldn't be trapped in a lie. Yes, my actions contributed to the torn ligaments in Larkin's knee, but I had just been using reasonable force to pull him down from the wall to prevent his escape. Yes, I had punched him to the face but had acted in self-defence because I was in fear of imminent assault. And with of course good reason because of the assault on me in the kitchen. In the end, it was my word against Larkin's, and barring overzealousness or dirty tricks, the Inspector would have to go elsewhere for a trophy.

In June Larkin was convicted in Court of assault police. In August the case against me was referred to the Crown Prosecution Service, and they decided that no charges should be brought. The disciplinary still hung over me and relied on a lesser burden of proof - that of the balance of probability. The cogs turned slowly, and I felt in limbo. I was climbing the walls in the CJU and needed to get out. It was a soul-destroying job which you didn't need to be a copper to do, but with a live complaint

I couldn't go anywhere else. My transfer back to Western Division had been put on hold and would sit gathering dust on the shelf until this debacle was over.

October came and I fell into a funk. Annabel had returned to University and the house was empty. The 18th was Beth's birthday and the screws of grief tightened. Work was miserable and my complaint was still unresolved. I had felt confident that it would be found unsubstantiated, although increasingly in my black mood, I envisaged standing in front of the Disciplinary Panel with my head bowed low. Starkly alone, experiencing a feeling of otherness as the word "Dismissal" was said.

One morning I sat on the side of the bed in my pants and couldn't move. I had to get ready for work, but I just sat there gazing at the chest of draws, a feeling of ennui draining me like an open tap. After what seemed like a while, I picked up the phone and reported sick with stress.

I lounged around all day binging on Netflix documentaries and episodes of Narcos. A little after four o'clock I mustered just enough willpower to workout, though my heart wasn't really in it. I stuck on some tatty, mismatched workout gear and went into the garage. I set the timer for thirty minutes and started off in front of the heavy bag with light, patting flurries to imaginary rib lines and jaw lines. I felt sluggish and it was tough going yet I stuck with it.

Eight minutes in and I forced myself through the gears and ramped up the intensity. I shelled the bag with heavy guns, slamming my fists into familiar indentations. The barrage was brief, dying off to nothing jabs and empty rights. I glanced at the clock – twenty minutes fourteen seconds remained. It is too long today, too long to go when you are running on fumes. I quit, and what was meant to lift me up drops me further down.

To preserve a modicum of respect I waited till five o'clock. Then I cracked open a bottle of Old Peculiar ale and got to the business of drinking – that I felt like doing. I ended four bottles and then eyed the whisky. Old Peculiar was a slow conversation, whereas whisky with its abrupt manner got to the point, and I was fond of getting to the point.

I had a Bulleit Rye Frontier whisky that I had taken a liking to and I poured a large glass. I had the iPad hooked up to the Bose and listened to a Spotify playlist featuring Kasabian, Bryde, The Pixies, U2, Public Enemy, Grinderman, Queens of the Stone Age, Big Black, The Cult and others. With my drink sloshing in my hand I danced badly, sung worse, shadow boxed and paced the length of my kitchen.

I threw whisky down my throat, made arguments and lamented my mistakes. I ran through ideas, old longings and thwarted ambitions. I thought about quitting the job and starting a business, about becoming a boxing coach at my local amateur club where I worked out, and other fanciful schemes. But what of the moment, what could be done now without any barrier or delay – there was Iceland, the once shared dream of Iceland. The carousel stopped and it became poignantly real – I would go. The following morning ruffled and croaky I went to the travel agents and booked whatever last-minute deal I could get.

CHAPTER 5

I wait for her to ask and consider what I would and wouldn't do. Most of what I imagine has me crossing the line, and even in my wayward mood I begin to have second thoughts. First among them was the fight, and I ran over what had occurred and tried to find lines that led back to me. On the plus side I was anonymous to them, there hadn't been any prior aggravation, and it had been over quick and clean. I had no marks or injuries, and if I washed my hands thoroughly there would be no chance of any blood or other DNA on mine - so forensically I had no worries. There were no witnesses that I saw, and though CCTV was a possibility it would be hard to get identification. However, if there were enough CCTV cameras I could be tracked through the city and perhaps to the hotel. Of course, all that would be an irrelevance if Marcus and Adam choose not to go to the police. And why would they go to the police after they had attacked a woman with the intent of stealing from her? or were they taking back something that belonged to them?

Then the penny dropped, I could be connected and that was through Toni. They knew Toni and Toni knew my name and where I was staying. The hotel had my full name and my travel company booking reference. If I was unlucky, and one of them didn't get up and was stretchered off to the hospital; if that was the case, and the Reykjavik PD came sniffing around, it would be best to tell the truth and justify what I did.

I then realized that I had been staring vacantly at my boots for half a minute. I brought my eyes up and Toni is finishing saying something that I hadn't heard. She then asks,

"Would you see me back to my hotel? I've hired a car and will be heading out onto to the Ring Road tomorrow."

"Yeah sure."

I eye the airport whisky; it is a perfect honey brown against the bedside light. I grab its neck and stop myself from taking a belt straight from the bottle. I pinch up two hotel coffee mugs with the other hand and place them on the table. I look at Toni and she nods. Not for her to think I am a lush I pour sensible measures and I sip instead of glug.

I give her one of my soft-shell fleeces; it is obviously too big but worn over her own with the sleeves rolled back it could pass. Toni doesn't have a small head, and with thick hair the other woollen hat I had brought fits her. I put a couple of layers on and leave my coat in the room. I figured Marcus hadn't seen much of me and Adam hadn't seen me at all, so I hand Toni my scarf and she wraps her face like an outlaw - northern extremes made it easy to conceal your identity.

"Where are you staying?" I ask.

"The Leifur Eiriksson."

I get reception to order a taxi and just after midnight we take off for the hotel. It is in the centre of Reykjavik, though in the opposite direction to the route we had walked. I get out of the cab and Toni pays the driver. The night air is harsh and my breath smokes upwards like a chimney. The Leifur Eiriksson is a four storey white building with large panel windows above the entrance, and a dormer extension protruding from the roof. Outside a bare black tree stood stark against the whiteness, its crooked branches like cracks in the building.

"Come on up," said as more of an instruction then an ask, her pale blue eyes lingering on mine.

I waver and then weaken, my legs moving while my mind still wrestles with itself. We get to the second floor and I am still telling myself to turn around, while surges of adrenaline run amok through my body. Outside the door, last chance to retreat, my body haywire with adrenaline. Toni takes my hand, a shiver of electricity shoots down my spine and I feel as weak as a lamb.

She slowly leans in and kisses me softly, her ample lips enveloping mine. I tremble with want and sin, the door opens, and I am led in.

I awake with a muggy head and a momentary dislocation of where I am. I roll over and Toni is asleep on her side next to me. I experience a tinge of guilt, but for what? I hadn't cheated, unless you could cheat your past. I am tired of beating myself up, so it is time I drop my baggage and look forward to the unknown.

I am struck by her attractiveness. I had been the night before, but this had been caught up in the whirl of booze, intrigue and violence. Now in the sober stillness of the early morning I fully appreciate her beauty. Not conventional beauty, I was never really into that, I like strong features: a prominent nose, a gap in the front teeth, a curl in the lip. Toni has a good Italian nose with a light dusting of dark freckles either side and a kinked, fat lipped mouth – if she had been a redhead she would have ticked all my boxes.

I dig her figure: it is curvy and firm like she works out hard, but isn't hung up about what she eats, which is a lot like me except I also don't much care what I drink either. I am definitely older than her, yet not by too much. She is around the forty mark and looks like she has had an eventful life, so she could be a couple of years younger. Like cars It wasn't always the age that mattered but the miles put on the clock, and I had done a few hard miles myself. I'm curious what kind of life she has lived and that I probably will not get to find out. I imagine that it had seen a fair share of turbulence, and for the base of this presumption there is Marcus. Psycho Marcus could be an unpleasant aberration in an otherwise steady existence, but I suspect that he is a bad card in a mixed hand.

Toni stirs and pulls her right arm from underneath the pillow and I can see what I had only glimpsed the night before. My imagination had not done it justice; I have seen bigger tattoos but nothing resembling this outside of a tattoo magazine. A mighty Kraken breaking the surface of a tempestuous ocean, the terrible tentacles wrapped around a large wooden sailing ship crushing it to pieces. The artistry is magnificent, the choice of permanent depiction fascinating; I mean what does it say about a personality, who they are: something, nothing or everything. Toni opens her eyes and I suddenly try to look like I am doing something other than watching her.

"Good morning," I say quietly, smiling.

"Good morning tiger," she replies with levity.

I laugh, it had been awhile.

"I could kill a coffee," she said with a longing I can relate to and then asks,

"Do you want one?"

"Yeah, thanks."

Toni rolled out of bed to her feet in one fluid motion and I see more ink on the back of her right shoulder. It is the head of a red faced Japanese style demon with yellow teeth, eyes and horns, its nostrils flared and mouth agape in fury. It glares at me, daring me to fuck with it as Toni gets the kettle going. My eyes are hungry for her and I snatch the opportunity to feed them.

She has sexy arched feet with black polished toenails, and a chain and rose tattoo on top on her right foot. Her calves are sculpted, and on the back of the left one there is a vivid green hand grenade with a skull imposed on it. She possesses the sturdy thighs and ass of a sprinter leading to an archaic compass tattoo at the base of her back. Her waist has a bit to spare and this adds a womanly softness to an otherwise taut physique. Her arms and shoulders are nicely toned though less developed than the legs; and covering the left upper arm is a tattoo of two flaming dice tumbling from a shot glass. I toy with the images and what they mean together. Intuitively it speaks to me of vice, risk, chance and the thrill of the three; that life is a gamble with an ambivalence to what is good and bad for us.

The kettle reaches a noisy boil.

"How do you take it?"

"Strong, plenty of milk, no sugar."

Beth knew how I liked it, and for her I used to scoop up the sugar and tap it back to get it just under half a spoon. Would she learn about me and I her, or does it fizzle out this morning in a few uncomfortable exchanges? It would be fine as it is – a great one-night stand, a true novelty for me after my swan like relationship with Beth. There is I sense something else in play, a shift from the old me, from my heavily regulated life towards something else. I get out of bed and take a coffee off Toni trying to recall the last time I had drunk coffee naked. I feel a little self-conscious about it and suck in my padded out six pack. The feeling is relegated by the sight of her augmented breasts in light and I am dumbstruck by their rounded perfection. And now I see what I had felt last night - a gold bar piercing through the left cherry that she had encouraged me to tweak.

"So! ... are you up for continuing our holiday romance?" she solicits in a voice sounding like Kathleen Turner on heat.

"Yeah ... I'm up! for it," I reply flirtatiously.

"I can see that."

Her eyes dropping low and then back to mine, her left hand tantalizingly poised on her hip like a sultry gunfighter. Above the coal polished nails, the base of a winter tree rising up her side, its ink black branches reaching like skeletal fingers for two ravens circling above. I don't have tattoos, but these made want to get some.

"Pretty inked aren't I?"

"Your tattoos are spectacular, a cut above the ordinary," I say appreciatively thinking about all the cheap, ghastly botch jobs I'd seen on the sink estates back home.

"I told you last night I wasn't like most people," she smiled and flicked an eyebrow again.

"I thought that you were joking, but I guess you were right." I pause a second, "If you are going on a trip around the island I'd like to come with you."

She doesn't skip a beat,

"Good if I get stuck in the mud you can push me out."

Cameron Bell

"I'll do some pushing now," I said with a wolf's grin and putting my coffee down I sweep her up and onto the bed.

CHAPTER 6

We set out in the Toyota RAV4 a little after 8 o'clock. The night faint and ebbing to a grey woollen sky. Toni has smuggled some Danish pastries from the buffet, and we eat them on the move. Toni drives with a pastry in hand, flakes falling into her fleece, and I eating mine grease up the screen of my phone navigating back to the Storm. Traffic is light, and the tall cranes dotted around the city are idle; there is building work everywhere - Reykjavik is city on the up.

Toni parks outside of the hotel and I run out and up to my room. I hastily pack my travel case and entertain the notion that Toni might not be there when I get back down. I have a bad dose of occupational suspicion which bleeds out into other areas of my life. I expected lies and assumed the worst of people. I know I am jaded, though I hope not irrevocably so. I brush my teeth and the bathroom mirror tells its tale. My eyes droop wearily and are underscored by darkness. My hair dark brown and wavy and always a fraction longer than most coppers has strands of white, the short beard too is flecked and uneven. I had seen a lot worse for my age, but I am not one of the better ones – a self-pampering metrosexual I am not.

I spit out and finish up. I check the room over for missed stuff, sling my light travel bag over my shoulder, pick up the case and exit the room. I hurry down the stairs anticipating an empty parking bay and see a taxi where she had been parked. I drop my case and feel a deluge of disappointment. Oh well, a player will play I thought. A car horn sounds from across the street and Toni is waving to me out the window. I pick up my case, the breath of relief a portent of trouble ahead.

We drive east out of the city passed rows of drab factory units and glass fronted retail outlets with garish signs. The outskirts contain mostly bland housing developments that are new and grey, and a poor contrast to the colourful corrugated fronts of old downtown. What set it apart from other cities is the lack of pollution and grime; apart from the graffiti it is clean and uncluttered, with open space and the absence of decay. It is the antithesis of my home town Port Talbot: a dirty steel town by the sea, a town of smoke and steam, of orange sulphur skies and tar stained sand. A town of poverty and pawn shops, bookies and pound stores. A sick town of pasties and fat filled leggings, of tappy walking sticks, smoker's coughs and busy chemists. A town of bedsits and Staffy dogs, broken families and needle driven oblivion. I saw the bad but there was the good. There had been a great deal of investment in face-lifting the train station, developing the seafront and building a super-sized comprehensive school, and the town is presentable in places; but for me all the bad that I had witnessed had tainted the good, like a stench you can't get rid of however much you clean.

We reach the open road and head north: houses stretched out from one another and became more individual, and wild Icelandic ponies ran the green fields in between. Mountains white capped and marbled with snow stood impressively in the distance. Traffic thinned out becoming more sporadic, and we passed a couple of strange structures erected at the side of the road warning motorists that there is danger to be found in these vast stretches. These were steel frames holding aloft two smashed cars in simulated collision, with a number on a Christian cross beneath denoting the number of fatalities.

"So where are we heading?" I ask.

"Ah that would spoil the surprise," Toni replies.

"A magical mystery tour around Iceland then. Will there be any hidden Easter eggs to find?" I scoff.

"There might be," and Toni lets out a self-knowing chuckle. "There will be if I'm right."

A silly joke which was not perhaps a joke, or a joke returned. I join in, I enjoy abstract humour.

"What ... actual Easter eggs ... are we looking for a giant white bunny with a sack then?"

"Not quite."

Toni takes her eyes off the road and her face moves through a series of mischievous expressions. She is playing with me and enjoying my confusion. I would have to work for the answer, if of course there is one. I speculate that if there is a purpose to this trip it isn't mundane.

"Not quite," I echo. "Okay you've succeeded in piquing my interest, and it has been piqued a lot since I met you."

I stroke my beard and ponder a moment before saying in a vaguely Holmes like manner,

"First scenario is that this is a travel game popular in Buffalo where the driver of a car bullshits the passenger to while away the time. The other scenario is that you are searching for something other than yourself on this lump of volcanic rock."

"Well! you got me, us Buffalonians love to bullshit," she says in a corny, confessional style.

"A bullshitter would say that though, we could still be playing," I laugh.

"Yes, we could."

I am not at all sure, and I guess I will have to wait to find out.

I notice the petrol tank is a third full.

"We're going to have to stop at the next petrol station, they are few and far between on this route."

"There's a bag of munchies in the back, help yourself and pass me a coke would you?"

I turn in my seat and reach back for the yellow shopping bag on the rear seat. It is a Bonus bag with a pink pig emblem – Bonus is the closest Iceland has got to a pound shop. There are four bottles of cola and I retrieve two, handing one to Toni. It is warmer than I would like, but I am far short on my daily caffeine intake and coke is always good for a hangover.

In my trouser pocket my phone vibrates. I wriggle in the seat and pull it out of my jeans; I have a text message. It is from Paul Spender a Detective Sergeant that I used to work with when we were both plain clothes cops on the Drugs Team in Neath. He had gone onto better jobs and I hadn't. We had got on, but after going our separate ways we had not kept in touch outside of chance meetings in work.

"Hi Will, hope you are well. I thought you would want to know that Chris Stillman died in a motorcycle accident on Thursday. The funeral is yet to be arranged and we're having a collection for a wreath."

I re-read it, death had been distilled to a text. It didn't seem real looking down on it on my phone. Chris Stillman was a tank and the best officer to have at your side when things got ugly – period. A former prop forward for Aberavon Rugby Team, he was a thick square man with practically no neck and a crudely carved block for a head. He had massive strength and could carry a fourteen stone man by the belt like a suitcase - and I had seen him do it. Damn! I thought, why does death always have to take the good ones.

We had worked together in Cwmavon on a Community Action Team and were a rough pair. We really made our presence felt in the Afan Valley and the local crims were scared shitless of us. We always liked filling our van up and used to laugh that a day without a prisoner was like a day without sunshine. The two of us certainly made a dent in the local crime figures, and many crims stopped fucking around on our patch and offended elsewhere.

Chris was good fun too and we'd mess about in Cwmavon Nick; an old police house that was with the other half of the team we shared it with all our own. Chris would pick up roadkill and stick it in my locker, and I pulled shit like putting itching powder in his boots, or salt in his coffee. On shifts when the four of us worked together we'd play football inside the station, and there would be bedlam with files and fire extinguishers getting knocked everywhere.

I realize now that those two years were the best of times and the happiest I'd be in the job; because the police is like a desert of shifting sands, an unsettling job of change and movement. Sure enough, the team was centralized at Port Talbot, then its remit and priorities changed, then reduced and ultimately disbanded. We all went off to other roles and I foolishly sought promotion. Chris was one of the few guys I'd worked with that I kept in contact with, and we would regularly go mountain biking together on the Afan Valley trails or meet up in Swansea for a pint and a curry.

I have a collage of memories with one that stands out among the rest, that summed the man up. It is fragmented and a little blurred or enhanced in places, but that's how memories are.

02:09 Saturday 9th September 2007.
Station Road, Port Talbot.

I scope the street.
Jimmy's Bar is kicking out.
I watch as they spill out in dribs and drabs milling around on the pavement, drinking their unfinished bottles in the amber glare of a town centre night.
Slack faced scumbags with vacant eyes, with bug eyes and grinding jaws. Cocky and spiteful, borderline criminal and criminal, twats and wasters almost to a man and woman.
I know them, they know me.
Shouts across the street, horse play, girls over shoulders, queues for taxis; I watch and wait for it to happen.
People standing in the road, people slobbering over kebabs, people heaving up their guts in shop doorways.
I tremble and kick the adrenaline out of aching feet.
Young tearaways on small stunt bikes and repainted mountain bikes, half-dressed girls with sore feet carrying their shoes, those that have pulled snogging and groping in dark recesses.

I look for trouble: face offs and straining necks, stabbing fingers and people being dragged away.
I wave at a passing panda and check my watch: 02:13 off at three - If I'm lucky.
Eyes back to Jimmy's and to the bulk of drug dealer Lee Pike stooping into a silver Citroen. I take down the registration plate for an intel. log later.
Then it flares - at the open door of a black cab two guys thrash and jerk into the road, punching, grabbing, stumbling.
I move, PC Chris Stillman behind me, towards two bodies rolling in the headlights of a halted car.
We sink our hands into the struggle and separate them.
I pull up the younger one: sun bed and highlights his flip flops in the road.
I take him to the pavement.
Aftermath: torn shirt, split lip, hysterical girlfriend.
"I'm going to kill the cunt!"
I look unimpressed, feel unimpressed; Chris at my shoulder,
"Minor injuries and custody are full, next drop off is Merthyr."
Enough said.
"No, you're not, you're going home."
I tune them out and keep talking, moving them towards a taxi I've flagged.
The blood is up, stirred monkeys in a zoo, bouncing off the walls, bouncing off each other - contagion.
I hear a bottle smash behind me, pig yelled from across the street.
Them hating me, me hating them.
Fucking Port Talbot.
Another fight breaks out and careers into the crowd knocking over a girl.
Two involved, with others from the sides sniping cheap shots.
Bear pit.
Head pulled down and smashed with a fist, smashed with a fist again and again.
I'm running.
Man bent over, face coming apart - there for the kill, the pack baying,

closing in.

I'm too late.

A two am warrior emerges from the left and detonates a knee off the bent man's head - contorted face snapped back across the shoulders, legs giving way, his face splatting into the pavement.

Must stop the kicks, the stomps, the hospital bed finishers.

Calls from the crowd, the assassin turns, flinches - is hit with a tackle.

He struggles, twisting, straining and shouting to stay standing, but I dig my grip in tighter around his waist and drive.

The sick orange lights, the cracked grey pavement, a line of blurred faces - spinning as we crash.

I'm on top - his teeth bared, arms poles to my neck.

Remember the cameras.

I break them; flip him over - his face in the cracks, cuffs out.

"Get the fuck off him!"

Jeers, gobs of spit, something at my back - simmering ready to boil over.

In the bear pit.

Fucking Port Toilet.

Fighting for his arms amid cartons and chip paper.

I screw a hand in to his chest and wrench one out and I jam it up his back.

"I'm getting this."

A skinny, shaven headed Scrote with tribal tatts named Luke Parsons is squatting down in front of me, his mobile pointed at my head; the small bad toothed hole in his pinched face having a go at a grin.

Straight in on my shit list.

"Stop resisting, you are under arrest for assault."

I snap on a cuff and tweak.

"Give me your hand!"

It comes.

"You're fucking hurting me!"

And with that it boils over into a bloody mess.

I'm knocked, grabbed, pulled, beer splashing on my neck and cheek.

Buffeted like a small boat I go over.

A trainer skims my face.
"Stamp the pig cunt!"
Another comes in, now blood is in the water.
They rain in – a free-for-all on a downed copper.
My vision shakes like a badly held camera and I can't get traction.
I hear a roar.
"Get back .... get back!"
The crowd buckles and bodies fly, jack-knifing and colliding off one another.
Stillman shoulders, Stillman shoves, Stillman hurls them out of the way.
Stillman is over me, his Asp scything space, smashing hands and whacking thighs of those too slow or stupid to get out of the way – Stillman the barbarian laying slaughter to the shitbags of Station Road.
I get up unhurt, and the rats run as a police van revs around the corner and stops in the middle of the street, blue lights pinging off the shop windows and hairy assed coppers jumping out.
I then hear Stillman say in that gruff Ammanford voice, a proper Welsh voice.
"Is that your prisoner Willsy running down the road? You'd better get after him, you know I don't run."

Tragic, fucking tragic; tears well in my eyes, I rub them, and they sting causing me to blink uncontrollably. I breathe out and try to hold it together; I've known this woman for two minutes and it doesn't feel right blubbering in front of her.
"You're upset what's wrong?"
No point in denying it and I didn't want to tell her another lie.
"Just had a text telling me that an old friend of mine has suddenly passed away."
"Oh, I'm sorry to hear that," and Toni put her hand on my thigh and gave it a squeeze.
I force a smile and said with a slightly quavering voice something I felt but ought not to have said.
"Life is pretty dreadful really."

"I suppose it is, sooner or later. It's just something you've got to accept and move through, or otherwise you're dead before you are dead. Death is not the greatest loss in life. The greatest loss in life is what dies inside of us while we live," she said matter-of-factly, though to my tender ear it sounded glib and something you'd get out of a self-help book.

"You're quite the philosopher."

"Yes, amongst many other things. Stick with me kid and you'll learn something."

Toni winked and made a pistol with her index finger and thumb. She tilted her hand and made a clicking sound inside of her mouth with her tongue. I am beginning to see that phoney self-aggrandizement is her schtick.

"Do you often steal lines from movies cowgirl?"

"Occasionally, the rest I get from books, records and toilet walls."

"Touché," I reply knowing I'd met my match and in the midst of the banter I forget I am sad; however, this is short lived, and the sun soon goes back behind the clouds.

I think about what she had said; there are the dead all right, the just found in bed dead, and the bloated black sack of maggots dead, and many other gruesome types of dead: train track shovel up the pieces dead, own dog eat your head dead, and they bear no resemblance to the living. No, you aren't dead before you are dead, there is something in between - there is the dead ... there is the dead and the drowning. I think it through because I have the need to put handles on things even if they don't always fit.

A swimmer with strong strokes making headway in a calm sea, having direction and feeling buoyant. Then travails: capricious currents, fickle weather, an unseen squall gathering on the horizon. Fatigue creeps in. Anxiously treading water, drifting from the shoreline – struggling, sinking, drowning. Into deep cold waters, into dark depths where lines blur and break - and the person is lost. Except of course that some poor buggers could never swim to begin with and were drowning from the start.

"Will."

I snap out of it,

"Yeah."

"We're getting low on gas, check out where the nearest gas station is, we might have to go off the route."

The RAV had only had a third of a tank at the start of the journey and we really should have filled up before leaving Reykjavik. I check google maps on my phone and there is a small town called Borgarnes three kilometres ahead of us. I put the name into Wikipedia and find that it has a gas station, swimming pool and a museum.

"We're good, there's a town just up ahead of us where we can fill up."

I want to leave my sullen thoughts and get on to a lighter conversation, and Toni beats me to it.

"So, I've been wondering, did you used to be a boxer or something?"

"Yeah, and in a way I guess I still am."

"How can I say this sensitively ... I can't. Aren't you too old at forty five to be taking punches to the head?"

"Well I only boxed seriously as an amateur to my mid-twenties. Then I started a career and got married and let it slide. I still kept in shape at the club and sparred with the guys, then for fun I got involved in the white-collar boxing scene. It's like exhibition boxing and we raise money for good causes."

"When you were serious were you any good or were you a bum?" she says cheekily.

"Pardon me ... a bum, no I was never a bum and that is such an Americanism. Actually, I was pretty decent, not great but I could mix it with those that were. I won a Welsh Amateur title three times at middleweight and was a runner up on two other occasions. Two of three times I qualified as Welsh champion for the British championship I got put out straight away in the semi-finals - got beaten by a lad from the army and a Scot named Darren McKenzie who went onto to win a bronze in the Olympics.

My last run at it I stopped an Irish boy in the semi and reached the final. I fought the same Scotsman McKenzie who had defeated me the previous year. He boxed my ears off like he did before, but I caught up with him in the last round and dropped him with a body shot. He rose at eight and clung on for the last twenty seconds to get his hand raised after the bell. My limitation at that level was that I lacked finesse. I could punch holes in people who stood in front of me, though I was often frustrated and outclassed by slick boxers like McKenzie who knew how to hit and move.

My favourite thing about boxing now is the heavy bag. I love the heavy bag and use it as much as other people run. I can tell that you work out quite a bit, what do you like to do?"

"I do CrossFit two to three times a week. I hit the Workouts of The Day as hard as I can, though I'm not into the whole Paleo eating thing. I tried it and after two days I wanted to eat my own arm. I like pizza and I like beer."

"No right-minded individual doesn't," I said.

CHAPTER 7

The Borgarfjarðarbrú bridge lays ahead and reaches over the fjord to Borgarnes. It is a long, simple concrete bridge propped up low above the water. This small town which is really no more than a village, sits neatly on a short peninsula. The roofs of the buildings are a patchwork of colours, and the buildings themselves are large and independent of one another. Standing on a low hill above the town is its notable structure: a white church with a slender tower that forms to a black point like a wizard's hat.

We cross over the bridge, the water below a ripple-less grey, while great swathes of the sky fill with black overbearing cloud, swollen and imminent. Off the main street there is an N1 petrol station with a huge forecourt and a café. We stop and I fill the RAV with diesel and make sure that I'm the one to pay. Toni excuses herself to the ladies to freshen up and I park the RAV in a space.

We meet back up in the café and Toni has already ordered a couple of lattes. We sit at a pine coloured table facing each other. Looking over her shoulder through the large window I can see in the near distance, a range of jagged toothed mountains, topped by a brooding bank of dense bruised cloud. I stir my coffee and comment,

"The heavens are going to open up any minute."

"Looks that way."

I take a breath and say with a smile,

"So, are we there yet?"

"What are you nine?" she replies throwing back her head in a mocking laugh.

"Sometimes, don't you know that boys never really grow up," and it occurs to me I was paraphrasing something that Beth had said to me many times.

"And don't you know that girls never grow out of teasing boys."

She fixes my eyes with hers and the lips strike a note of attraction, moving alluringly into an uneven smile. I decide not to press the question even in humour. It doesn't really matter where we are going, and perhaps it is best to just switch off and go along for the ride. Switching off is good and I needed to do more of it, however it is no different to telling an alcoholic he should drink less.

The bigger question is why Marcus and his buddy had followed Toni to Iceland? If he wanted to get to her surely he could have done it with far less difficulty back home. He would only have to wait up on Toni at her tattoo parlour and there would be an opportunity. The trouble with making deductions is you must be sure of the facts that you are deducing from. If the source material is questionable so are all deductions. The only fact I could be certain of is that I heard one of them demand that Toni hand over something - but what? It had to be something valuable or incriminating, and something that had to be obtained with some urgency. There are several possibilities: a code or password of some kind, a key, a photograph, a document, a recording, drugs, money or precious stones perhaps.

"A penny for your thoughts?" she said.

I hesitate - a man should rarely tell a woman what he is really thinking. Thoughts had to be edited before spoken. I dissemble wanting to know more about my Femme Fatale.

"I was going to ask if you'd always been a tattoo artist or if you had done other things?"

Toni took a deep breath and then answered,

"My life in two minutes. The last nine years I've been in the ink trade, five working for someone else, and four out on my own. Before that I was a nurse, and before I was a nurse I was a dancer.

As a teenager I went to an academy of performing arts and

majored in contemporary dance. After graduation I went to New York and got work in off Broadway productions in the chorus line. Some of the productions toured and one even made it to Broadway for a bit. I auditioned for dozens of commercials and managed to get a couple, and I featured a few times in hip-hop music videos as a backing dancer. I was enjoying what I was doing and making a good living from it until I got injured. I hurt my Achilles tendon and it just wouldn't heal properly. I didn't have the money for surgery to correct it and it kept giving me problems; in the end I couldn't dance to the level that was needed and I had to stop.

So, at twenty-four years of age I moved back to Buffalo and tended bar at The Union Pub for a nearly a year, until I figured out what I was going to do next. I needed to re-train but earn at the same time and nursing seemed like a good option. I nursed in E.R. for the next seven years, never really liking it and I felt unfulfilled. The carnage and working conditions wore me down, and I became depressed and dependent on Sertraline."
Nibbling her bottom lip, she looks down at the table as if processing some hurtful memory, then continues.
"To add to this, around the same time I had a short, stupid marriage to a paramedic that was screwed from the start. We both had affairs, and Brandon the guy I got with is a tattooist. It developed into more than a fling and I ended the marriage. I moved in with him and grew interested his work; there are tattooists and there are tattoo artists and Brandon is an artist. I mean his designs and inkmanship are incredible, and he has done all my work. I wanted to learn, and he took me on as an apprentice, and I quit nursing.

Over the next five years I learned the craft and the business and became good in my own right. Over time our relationship cooled, and we became more friends than anything, and it felt like it was time to go it alone. So, four years ago I moved to a small city outside of Buffalo called North Tonawanda and opened a parlour … and that's me."

"Is it one of them cities that's really no more than a town?" I ask.

"Yeah small-town America, population 31,500. We just like to make things sound bigger than they are," she replies.

"Is that where you met Marcus?" I venture.

Toni rolled her eyes and made a nauseous gesture with her mouth.

"Yeah, and we'll leave that for another time. Anyhow, changing the subject, what about you, have you always been a firefighter?

I was faced by my own lie. I didn't like lying, unfortunately deceit is a necessary adjunct to the job. Criminals dealt in lies, and to be a wholly truthful person put you at a disadvantage – the dishonest bird catches the worm. But this is not one of those situations, and I had lied about what I do for a living because I am sick of it, and the stigma it often carried. People just treated you differently: they were wary of you, resentful of you, scornful of you, some were curious, a few sought to solicit favour, others had admiration, and the odd one would do you harm if they knew. The trouble is you couldn't stand aside from it – you wore the uniform and it wore you. I wanted just for one week to forget it all, and now what I thought was a casual conversation in a bar, was not.

I considered telling her the truth, but why spoil the fling. If perchance it grew to become more than that, then that would be the time for full disclosure. Until then I would be honest in all other respects bar that I am a Copper. I put my hand through my hair and began telling the story of my alternative life,

"For nearly all my working life yeah. After school I went to college, where I failed to distinguish myself. I spent too much time in the gym and the common room, and not enough in the library, and I left getting the grades I deserved. University was out, and so I moved through a succession of dead-end jobs. I worked part-time in a record store, drove a taxi for a bit, collected and cleaned cars for a car dealership, was briefly a bouncer in a nightclub, and eventually wound up through my uncle in the steel works.

I laboured in the blast furnace: it was dirty, hot and randomly dangerous and it clarified my thinking. I saw that I could spend the best years of my life in a smelly shit-hole, or that I could get out and get a career. The way I saw it with my qualifications I could join the army, the fire service or the police.

By this time, I had been seeing Beth for about two years and was completely smitten by her, so the army with its prospect of overseas postings was kicked into touch. That left the fire service and the police, and the fire service were the first to say yes. I joined at twenty-two and gradually worked my way up to become a Watch Manager.

Beth and I married two years after I joined, and we had two children together Nathan and Annabel. Funnily enough, it was Nathan that enlisted in the 1st Queen's Dragoon Guards known as the Welsh Cavalry, and Annabel who went to university to study law. They both have done what I couldn't, which is what you want for your children."

I had told Toni last night at the Gaukurinn that I am a widower, and I didn't feel the need at this stage to go into the unpleasant details. I sensed a sadness in Toni when I mentioned my children, and I made a mental note to steer clear of the topic.

"Speaking of services, my father was in the Navy, and he was stationed in Iceland through the late 70's and early 80's," Toni said.

I didn't understand whether her father was Icelandic or American, and vocalized my confusion "Really in Iceland as Ice .."

Toni interrupted,

"The United States had a naval air base at Keflavik. My father was a P-3 Orion crewman."

I pursed my lips, gave a gentle nod and I said,

"I did not know that."

"My father loved the country. In his free time, he would drive around the island exploring. He was a history buff and a keen metal detectorist. He would spend hours alone, scanning fields and beaches for Viking artefacts."

"He find anything?" I ask.

Toni laughs, an echo of a laugh from another time and place.

"Yes, a few boat nails, a coin, a cooking pot and a brooch."

"Didn't make him rich then?"

"No, but it did make him a friend, Jon Einarsson, and they corresponded with each other for nearly forty years."

CHAPTER 8

The wipers work frantically against the slashing rain which pounds the car in heavy sheets. Toni sits hunched at the wheel peering through the spattered windscreen, driving like at any moment the road is doing to disappear. Rain drops explode on the road creating a film of water that the tyres split and whish over.

Lights smudged against the misting glass emerge ahead. A beast of a transport truck driving to a deadline and skimming the white line roars past - its mass close and unnerving. I flinch, and the mangled car sculptures now have meaning – don't stray over the dividing line, do not take the weather lightly.

"Jeez that truck was close, he was over our side of the road!" I say, sitting back properly in the seat. Lorry drivers are a law unto themselves, do all sorts of things in their cabs whilst driving.

"Visibility is shit. We should stop somewhere and let it pass," Toni replies, looking rattled herself.

The downpour had started fifteen kilometres out of Borgarnes, and we had been travelling north along Route 1 at a snail's pace for the last thirty.

I hear a car horn. A single barp, followed by a longer one, two short ones and then a longer one. Toni checks the interior mirror, and I look over my shoulder through the rear windscreen. I see about two car lengths behind us, a large green four by four which looks like a Land Rover Defender with its hazard lights blinking. The horn sounds again in a Morse code pattern of barps.

"What does this prick want?" Toni exclaims irately.

I check the dashboard for warning lights and there aren't any, and the RAV4 doesn't feel or sound in difficulty.

"Car seems okay," I say.

Toni lowers the driver's window and waves the Defender on.

"Come on if you wanna pass, fucking overtake. Come on what are you waiting for!"

The Defender lays back, hazards blinking and horn blasting.

"He must want to warn us of something, wants us to stop," I say.

"Should we?" Toni asks in a tone suggesting that we should probably not.

"Broken bridge ahead or ulterior motive; I go with people are shit, every day of the week." I reply sardonically.

Then in a burst of speed the Defender darts into the opposing lane, overtakes, and crosses back over the white line in front of us. It slows and settles a length and a half ahead.

"What's he playing at?" I think aloud.

Is some idiot dicking around to break the boredom of the open road? And I remember, when age fourteen, riding my racer home one night along a stretch of deserted dual carriageway, and a car slowing alongside pushing me into the kerb. And then for no reason an arm shooting out the back window, trying to snatch the handlebars.

Red brake lights flash, and the back of the Defender suddenly magnifies in the windscreen, its tyres disappearing under the bonnet of the RAV. Toni rigid, pushing away from the steering wheel slams on the brakes and we skid towards a collision. We hit with a light but jolting bump, which does not activate the air-bags. We come to a stop, and with our rate of deceleration being more rapid, distance is created, and the Defender comes to a halt fifty yards further on.

I see the realization in Toni's face, as the Defender its wheels churning up water reverses. The Defender picks up speed and I brace myself for the impact. Toni floors the accelerator, and the wheels spin for traction. I watch powerless, my life in the hands of a maniac and a woman I barely know. The tyres then catch the road and the RAV lurches into an acute left turn, just in time to avoid the backward charge of the Defender. The RAV is now heading off road onto gravel and a ditch. Toni throws the steering into a hard right, and the rear swings out tearing up tufts of grass and small stones. The RAV fish-tails before straightening out and we cut back across the road, the engine straining raucously in first gear.

The Defender is on our tail, and Toni shifts up the gears accruing speed through the lashing rain. I look over my shoulder and the Defender is gaining on us. It is a bigger, sturdier vehicle used by the British Army and would come off better in any collision. We had to try and outrun it and to do so would mean taking risks. I thought what I could do as a passenger and other than phoning the police there is not much - it is down to Toni.
I look ahead as far as I can, and there is just the road and the grass beside it. The nearest village Buoardular is thirty kilometres away - so if I did call the police it would take too long for them to reach us.

The Defender surges behind us, and Toni her hands squeezing the life out of the steering wheel drives harder. I could see a bend ahead and Toni sees it too. It is a sweeping bend on a shallow slope, which in normal conditions would not pose a hazard, but with the heavy rain and high-speed pursuit it does.

"Slow down for the bend," I blurt, unsure if I had made the right call.
Toni's face contorts in anguish at having to make the least shit choice. She eases off the gas and drops a gear, and we approach the bend at a more sensible speed. The driver of the Defender takes a different gamble, and accelerating rams the back of the RAV as we enter the bend. The impact violently shunts the RAV through the bend and over the verge. I stretch my arms against the dashboard, and we bounce and rattle down the bank until running aground on a small tump of earth.

Toni sighs, a deep resigned sigh. She looks at me intently like I am her last hope on earth and says rapidly,

"Isafjordur, they're going to take me to Isafjordur. Find Jon Einarsson."

So, there is more, a scheme or enterprise of some sort that is unravelling fast.

"They haven't got you yet ... get out!" I said with as much steel as I could muster.

I grab the travel bag at my feet, fling open the passenger door and leap out onto thick boggy grass. I look behind, clutching the forlorn hope that they'd overturned and are trapped. No such luck - the Defender is perched precariously over on the verge - its doors open.

Two men are out, scrambling down the shallow hill, they have scarves around their faces and carry aluminium baseball bats. I could see by the nasty bleached hair that one of the men is Marcus, and he takes a diagonal course towards Toni's side of the RAV. I glance across to my right and Toni is running at a clip through the field away from the road.

The second guy who I assume is Adam makes for me. He is about my height, thickset on top, wide at the hips and pudgy in the arse, thighs and gut. He is swarthy skinned with a short receding hairline, and he is attired in red trail boots, black jeans and a black hoodie.

I estimate that if I run I could outpace him; he was the wrong shape and looked like he didn't have the cardio. Marcus would catch Toni though, and that mattered enough.

I'd been in some dicey situations and come out of them, although this time I couldn't see how I am not heading for the hospital or a hole in the ground. A glimmer in the gloom, is that Marcus had made a tactical mistake. He had split from Adam and gone for Toni, when he should have gone for me also.

Ten yards out Adam brings his run to a stride and hefts the bat over his right shoulder, his hands nervously kneading the handle as he advances. I shuffle backwards, holding my bag in front of me with both hands. I cower, and shaking my head

plead,
"Take her if you want, I won't get in your way."
In a guttural voice the masked man replies,
"No, you won't – period. I'm going to fuck you up six ways from Sunday for that sucker punch."

It is a matter of range and I watch it close. Judgement of range, control of range, each step like the ticking hand of a clock - until the time. I see the bat twitch in readiness for the strike and that is the time. I pounce, and from the chest, thrust the travel bag with both hands into flight at his head. I follow through with the momentum, my guard held high. Instinctively he brings the bat across to parry the bag leaving the bat un-cocked. The bag hits the ground and I am almost upon him.

He takes a step back and re-lifts the bat. I close in and the bat comes down at my range and not his. I block it above the handle with my left forearm and avoid the brunt of the hit as the mid-part strikes the top of my head. He raises the bat again and I get in around his waist, locking my hands together in an S grip. I pull them into the small of his back and bear hug him. He panic hits me to the side of my head with round edge of the handle, and cuts open my scalp. I ignore these scraping blows, get low, lift and steer him right into the side of the RAV.

"Marcus ... Marcus!" he shouts with a whiney pitch that is now far from guttural. He struggles to break free and continues to painfully stab my head with the handle of the bat. I release my grip and pin him to the car with my left shoulder, leaving a small gap to escape to his left. He takes the bait, and as he slides out I punch.

It is a short punch that travels no more than nine inches. The leverage learnt through ten or even perhaps twenty thousand repetitions on the heavy bag. A snap of the hips creates the torque that revs up through the torso, shoulder and finally the arm to the fist. The uppercut plunges into his solar plexus like a spade deep into soft soil. It feels that if I'd been able to hit him any harder I would have reached his spine. I let the shot sit for a second and I hear him emit something between a retch and a squeal. I pull back and his legs sag, and as he is going down I finish him with a short, bludgeoning right hook that smacks him flush on the nose. The back of his head bounces off the door of the RAV and he falls to prayer on his hands and knees.

Suddenly spooked by the realization that I could be blindsided by a bat, I do a three sixty and see that I am safe for the moment. I then do something that I had never done before; I take measure and deliver a hard soccer kick to the side of the man's head. His arms give way and he is out, face down in the mud and grass.

Rivulets of blood and water roll into my eyes and the rain seeps into my clothes. I feel strangely ebullient - a feeling derived from coming out on top of something that should have had me beat; but I am not out of the woods yet, the job is only half done.

I pick up the bat and go after Toni. The going on the boggy ground is difficult, with energy dissipating in slips and saves. Toni has got further than I thought. She has run to the end of the field where there is a gentle rise leading to a flat area of stone and short grass. The area is enclosed on the left by a bank of steep, slabbed rock, and sharply dropped away on the other side into a gorge.

Marcus is gripping Toni by the scruff of the hair with his left hand and holding the bat midway along the length with the right. His scarf is loose from his face and dangling from his shoulders to his thighs. Marcus is dragging her in the direction of the Defender, and Toni fighting his hand with hers is digging in her heels and pushing back. Marcus is looking back talking to her. I can't hear what he is saying, though I figure he is tearing strips off her with foul, excoriating words. He then leans his weight forward and pulls her along a few feet before she digs her heels in again and they stop. Marcus viciously pokes her hard in the stomach with the end of the bat, and Toni doubles over and drops to her knees.

Under the radar, I draw near and hear him scold her as he kicks her in the back of the legs.

"You're a cheating, lying, thieving whore. You're not running out on me again. We were in this together. Greedy fucking bitch wanting it all. You're getting nothing, but I might just let you live if you play your part."

Marcus shoots into a Karate stance and kicks Toni in the ribs, "keeeaaahhh!"

Toni rolls onto her side into a foetal position and squirms in the mud, dry-retching pain.

Marcus prances in a half-circle with the end of the bat cockily resting across his shoulder. When he comes about he sees me slogging up the rise. He skips back, the sadistic smirk still on his face. He throws his scarf off and warms up the bat, and says contemptuously,

"To the rescue hey. Is she paying you, or is she fucking you? I bet she's fucking you, hot between the sheets isn't she?" he smacked his lips. "What you don't yet realize is you dumb fuck, is she is ... fucking you!"

Marcus slowed and emphasized the last part of the sentence by breaking the word down into its syllables, and by grossly exaggerating his mouth.

"When she's got no further use for you, she'll dump you like garbage. That's what the bitch did to me. She told you lies, she told you why we're here, did she offer to cut you in? What line of bullshit have you fed him Toni? ... it doesn't matter, your fucking meddling ends here."

I wipe the blood from my eyes and settle my breathing. I had listened to what he said, much of it was vitriol, yet in there, there are probably grains of truth too. I could have done talking with the asshole for longer, but I didn't see it working out that way. We are going to fight, and it is likely to be for keeps, at least on his side. I would do enough; I had no doubt he would put me in a wheelchair or worse.

A grenade of adrenaline goes off in my gut and I feel its shivering tremors; and despite the pending violence, I appreciated the beauty of the spot where we are going to try to cave each other's heads in. I could hear the wash of a waterfall below and see the misty spray rising above. I take a deep breath,

"You are a prize cock. I've dealt with hundreds, and you're making your way into my top ten. Do you want to dance again?"

I let the words linger, I want him to lose his composure and rush. He doesn't bite, he chuckles and says haughtily,

"The fucktard speaks. You got lucky, you won't be lucky twice. Have you fought with swords before? I have, you're in for a treat."

Though it may have been bravado, a chill ran down my spine and a crack of doubt appeared. With the background in karate it is possible that he had practised with a Katana, or even done Kendo. I shut it out. So what, we are where we are and there was no opting out or going back. I know my way around a baton, understood leverage, and I know violence - let the dice roll.

I hold the bat in traditional slugger style and with a bladed stance edge forward. Marcus adopts a samurai's pose and holding the bat out in front of his lean six foot frame moves obliquely. The bat bobs, blood drips over my brow - both of us manoeuvring into the point of ignition.

Marcus lunges flexing his wrists, and the bat strikes out like a snake clonking against my forehead. I buzz and reel, I swing for the stands, if I would have hit I would have killed, but I do not. Marcus at angles, bending away from the blow, not in front of me, now at sixty degrees off the centre line. I go forward with the momentum of the swing, turn around and jump back to face him, and our positions are reversed. There is a wobble in my legs, and my head is fuzzy and hurts like a bastard.

He doesn't let me off the hook and comes in again. I let fly with a back swing to smash him on the way in, yet this time it is a feint. He is not there. He has aborted mid-attack and opened me up for a counter-strike. He springs forward, and the bat moves minimally from in front of his head into mine with alarming speed. With sickening impact, the hollow metal bat clunks off the left side of my head, and a curtain of night descends. I stagger back and the curtain recedes - and my senses are scrambled all to hell. I try to restore my balance, however my foal like legs disobey and I stumble and sway like a boxer about to be finished.

Through pixelated vision I see Marcus raise the bat above his head. I turn away and bend, shielding my head behind my left shoulder, and with a harsh Japanese cry, a powerful, diagonal blow thuds into the meat of it. Pain radiates along my arm and I am knocked and spun. I trip and topple over, put my hand out to break my fall, and continue falling.

CHAPTER 9

I half open an eye and close it. I slowly open it again and blink. I can see green lines, vertical and slanting underneath an off-white vagueness. At this moment I am no more than an eye attached to a muddled brain. I feel stone cold like part of the earth with no general sense of self. Pieces gradually come together, and I feel my form numb against the earth. I recognize the shapes to be grass and sky, and I am face down, spread in the position that I smacked the sodden, green ground.

I marshal my thoughts and command myself to move. The body is reluctant to respond, and I consider that perhaps I am unable to move, that I am trapped, or my spine is severed. I begin to panic, and the grid turns on throwing everything into gear.

Sluggishly, I peel my head from the cold, squelching mud and push myself up onto my knees. The bat is next to me and I use it to get to my feet. I have a headache, a sore shoulder and some cuts and bruises. I am colder that I have ever been. Then I think how easily Marcus did a number on me, how I failed Toni and I manage to pour salt on my own wounds.

It is still day, and the rain has eased to a light drizzle. I take in my surroundings: I am on a ledge about twelve feet each way, encroached on three sides by slabs of craggy, moss covered rock. In front of the ledge there is a twenty foot drop into a deeper part of the gorge. The waterfall gushes from my right at the higher point of the gorge, which is level to where I am standing. Looking up I have fallen roughly fifteen feet and will need to climb back up to get off the ledge.

Tapping my Fitbit, it reads 2:47; I have a couple of hours of light to get to the road and flag a driver down. I get my phone out from my front trouser pocket - it is undamaged, has a signal, though only has a twelve percent charge. In my other trouser pocket, I have my wallet containing a bank and credit card, ninety=four thousand Krona and my slightly bent specs. Everything else is in the bags.

I look for an easy route - I will need one; I am scared of heights and my hands feel like dead fish. There is a line that has some decent holds, it veers left midway and then straightens up. I bounce some of the stiffness out of my joints and breathe some heat into my hands and give it a try. The holds are slimy cold sucking out of my hands any restored warmth leaving them as articulate as claws. I am at pains to obtain an adequate grip, and to add to my woes my boots are too cumbersome for the smaller edges, and I struggle to get purchase on the rock. I get half way up and a rock comes loose, my foot slips, I drop and fall off the face. I land on my feet, compress, knee myself in the chin and finish on my ass.

I am sitting on soggy ground in already wet jeans and I am shivering. The soft-shell fleece I am wearing is water resistant, however the resistance has gone allowing the jumper to become wet in most places, and long-sleeved top underneath to become damp. My teeth chatter and I shiver uncontrollably. I realize that the situation is more serious than I first thought; that I am going downhill from hypothermia and could die here. The thought dwells and does not fill me with horror. From what I have read there are far more unpleasant ways to meet an end. There is a painless confusion as the body shuts down and an overwhelming desire to drift off to sleep. Instead of shitting the bed in a nursing home I would go out on my shield – like a Viking, a modern day one with a baseball bat instead of an axe. The thought amuses me, and I giggle a little. Of the two hundred and fifty or so deaths I had attended I had never been to one caused by exposure - I could be my first.

The headache I have from the bat is being replaced by one

caused from the cold; like when you gobble ice cream too quickly - except it is a whole lot worse, and it isn't going to go away - well it will if I die. I laugh again, it would be so easy to just lay back and let it happen. I would only have to not do anything and stress, grief, loneliness and all the other shittiness of existing would vanish. There are the children though, and they had been through enough grief. It would be selfish to lumber them with a frozen dead father in Iceland.

I haul myself up and get out the phone, and with my spatula hands I find my location on Google maps. I then open up a browser, and with difficulty and error search for and phone the Icelandic emergency number 112. An operator with near accent less English answers, and I follow her script providing her with my personal details and contact number. I describe my location using the RAV4 and waterfall as pinpoint flags. I then explain to her what has occurred and my current predicament. She informs me to keep moving, that help is on its way from Buoardular and to not make any further attempts at climbing.

I check the time, 2:59. What time did they shift change here? back home it would be 3 pm and no one would be in a rush to leave the briefing room and a nice brew. The other thing is who is going to respond to the call? – that is a lottery. I hoped it would be the keen, conscientious officer or medic that would keep looking, and not the lazy good for nothing uniform carrier clearing the call after mere minutes with, "Area search negative."

I pace back and fore vainly kicking and clapping the cold from dead disconnected limbs, feeling stiff like many of the rigored bodies I've rolled over. I think about trying to climb out again; that it would perhaps be a good idea to cover the bases. Just in case this area is waterfall city and they go to the wrong one. The drizzle ceases and I take some heart from it, though it is still gloomy with the sun buried behind the clouds. I conclude that it is probably worth giving it a go, and if I fall again I am unlikely to be hurt that badly.

Taking the same route, I gingerly fix onto the holds willing myself to stay on. I get to the point where I fell before and dig a boot into the hole left by the dislodged stone. I can barely feel my hands and my whole body complains from the effort, still I push, pull and grunt my way up to the top. At the edge on my knees I want to collapse, yet I raise myself knowing that if I stop I'm done.

I cross the arena of my defeat and allow the slope to motor weary legs. I flounder a bit on the soggy grass, but I keep putting one foot in front of the other and make progress. The RAV is still stuck on the tump and I dodder towards it.

On reaching it I get in and find the keys still in the ignition. With a clenched fist I say a silent yes and get the engine running. I turn up the heater to maximum and then reach behind for the goody bag. I grab a coke, and for the first time I don't mind it being warm. I pop the top and draw long, messy gulps. This is followed by a peanut butter chocolate bar which I have to open with my teeth. As the car heats up I shiver more but I am not worried because I have heat, food and a change of clothes. I thaw my hands enough to take off my jacket and jumper, then I warm awhile.

I think about what Toni and Marcus said and add it to what I know. Her father was a navy airman stationed here. He was into Viking history and metal detecting. He met an Icelander named Ron ... Arnasson or something who liked the same stuff, and they became lifelong pen pals. Marcus and Toni were in on something together and she bailed out on him. This something has got to do with this Ron fella and Isa ... Ina ... shit. My memory is like Swiss cheese and I fall back on my phone to figure it out. Into Google maps, type Iceland Isa and the top suggestion is Isafjordur - yes that is what she said. I press it and the screen zooms in far north west on the map – bingo, that was where we were heading, and that is where they are heading now.

With some warmth restored I alight from the RAV and go to open the boot. The back bumper is dented and the casings for both brake lights are smashed. The door is stiff to open but gives with a hard yank. Toni's case is gone, and mine has been left.

From it I pick a pair of pants, socks, black jeans, t-shirt, turtle-neck jumper, Helly Hansen coat and grey Sketchers. I undress and sit on the sill of the boot to change. I tread carefully to the passenger side selecting stones and clumps of grass to step on. My rucksack is still there, and I retrieve it and get back into the RAV from the passenger side. I open my bag and find that my passport and airline ticket are still in the travel wallet that Beth had bought for our holidays.

I have what I need to get home. Just tell the local police about the kidnapping, bumble around Reykjavik for a day or so, take a trip south to Vick to see the black beach, and then jet back to the U.K. I nod to myself to signal agreement with this plan. I'd put myself on the line and did all that I could to help her. The sensible option is to now walk away and let the police deal with it. She had led me down the garden path, albeit with my knowledge, but all the same there was deceit. In her defence, could she really have been honest? perhaps not. In any case I knew I was playing a dangerous game, and that was the reason I played it – there was nothing new there.

I have a look at the damage, and it makes me smile. My reflection in the visor mirror is a sorry sight. Half a face caked in dried blood and mud, the other side smeared with blood; hair dirt matted and brown and clotted with blood from the splits beneath. There is a haematoma on my forehead the size of a golf ball – fair play, it looks like I've been thrown through an assault course. The Instagram selfies will have to be put on hold - as if!

The opening sequence of the original *Get Carter* plays, and I answer the call.

"William Cutter," I enunciate in as clear English as my working-class Welsh roots will permit.

"William Cutter," the male Icelandic voice echoed.

"Yes, I am William Cutter."

"Good, I am Sergeant Magnus Sigurdsson of the National Police. I am twenty-five kilometres out of Buoardular and should be with you briefly. Can you say the bend that you drive off is about forty kilometres out of Borgarnes?"

"Yes, yes, a long bend with a decline ... downward slope the other side. I am back in the car at the bottom."

Good, I thought he wants to confirm information and be precise.

"In the car, is that right, no longer over the cliff?" he enquires.

"Yes, in the car."

"Are you injured?"

"Nothing much, lumps and cuts."

"Okay, and your girlfriend ... Tonya ... she is missing?"

"Kidnapped ... taken."

"Yes, okay, we'll be there in five minutes."

I had thought about standing on the bend and making it easier for them to find me, but I am too damn cold. I wait in the car with the heater blasting and doze off. And in this altered state between the conscious and unconscious reality blurs. Beth is walking away, and I am behind her. Astonished and overjoyed, I quicken my pace and she does not, yet she remains out of reach. I call out to her. She glances over her shoulder with an expression of indifference and continues walking. I run at full pelt, but it is as if I'm running underwater and Beth fades into the distance, into the murky beyond.

CHAPTER 10

I rouse with a start. There is tapping at the window, and a pleasant looking man in black fatigues is peering in.

"Mr. Cutter, it is Sergeant Sigurdsson."

I open the door and he wisely steps back further than he needs to. I climb out cautiously and keep my hands in view.

"I am glad to see you, I've been having a bad day."

"Yes, it looks that way," he replies in a kind, dulcet voice.

Sigurdsson is just shy of six feet tall and has narrow rounded shoulders, and the accentuated lower body of a dedicated cyclist. He is in his early thirties and has bright, inquisitive eyes. His fine brown hair is cut close at the sides, is longer and tousled on top and it flutters in the breeze. He is kitted out very similar to how I would be. He is wearing body armour with the word Logreglan in yellow on his right breast and the word police in yellow on his left. The epaulettes have yellow bars, though no shoulder number, and there is a round yellow insignia on each upper arm. He wears an utility belt carrying an extendable baton, an incapacitant spray of some kind, handcuffs, radio, and pouches maybe for a torch, Leatherman tool, pocket resuscitation mask etc., and like the British Bobby he does not routinely carry a firearm. The boots are tactical, and trousers are of the combat variety with large thigh pockets and two reflective silver bands around the calves.

To the left of him standing behind the RAV is a squat female cop, in her late twenties with thick blonde hair tied in ponytail. She is looking at the registration plate and is speaking Icelandic on the radio. She then says something in Icelandic to Sigurdsson. Sigurdsson nods and says,

"Mr. Cutter did you hire this car?"

"No Toni did."

"Toni?" his top lip wrinkling and head askew, "Not Tonya?"

"There is no Tonya, there is Toni with an I, and she is a woman."
Third parties, radio communications, different language, there
had been errors passing information.

"Okay, who is Toni?"

That is a good question I thought.

"Toni is a woman I met last night at the Gaukurinn bar in Reykjavik. She is an American, a tattooist, and she is here on vacation.
We hit it off and I stayed the night with her at her hotel. She told
me she was taking a trip around the island and I asked to go with
her. I'm afraid I don't even know her last name."

Sigurdsson frowned and said,

"I see ... What happened?"

"Well, her ex-boyfriend Marcus and his friend Adam ran us off
the road. Marcus chased Toni over to the waterfall, and Adam
attacked me with a baseball bat. I got the better of Adam and
went after Marcus and Toni. Marcus caught Toni, and we fought
with baseball bats and I lost. He knocked me over the cliff and
when I came around they were gone. They are in a green Land
Rover Defender and I think they are taking her to Isafjordur," I
explain mangling the place name.

"Mmmm why do you say that?" he said quietly with a hint of
incredulity.

"Because she told me they would."

"When?"

"Just after we were bumped off the road. She said they're going
to take me to Isafjordur, find Ron Somethingsson. Obviously
not Somethingsson ... a name ending in son."

"That is of little help, nearly all Icelandic men are a son - Magnússon, Björnsson, Njálsson, he replies with a polite dismissiveness.

My headache is bothering me, it has sharpened, and I am feeling a little dizzy. I'd been amped up, battered and frozen and now I am beginning to crash with fatigue.

Sigurdsson gently nodded, which most people would see as a sign of encouragement, but I perceive it to be an indication of scepticism. I might be wrong, though I had done the same.

"When this happened were you driving?"

"No Toni was."

"Have you drunk alcohol today?"

"No."

This is starting to veer off course. The female cop is receiving and transmitting information on her personal radio. She then relays something to Sigurdsson who says to me,

"Mr. Cutter we've had a report of a Toyota driving ..."

He pauses thinking of the word and does a slithering gesture with his hand mimicking the movement of a snake. The word seemed to escape him, and he settles for,

"All over the road. We've then had another report that a rented Toyota RAV4 has been stolen from here by a man named, William."

Sigurdsson held my eyes for a reaction.

"Really! No ... no."

I shake my head and point to my pregnant forehead.

"This was caused by a baseball bat."

I feel a bit light headed and lean against the side of the RAV.

"That could have been caused by the accident, maybe you don't wear a seatbelt and bang your head."

Sigurdsson tilted his head again.

"I'm going to ask that you take a breath test and drug saliva test to see if you are drink or drug driving. Follow Constable Grimsdottir's instructions."

Constable Grimsdottir assembled the breathalyser and explained the procedure asking when I last had a drink or a cigarette. I tell her last night and never. Then she presents the device for me to blow into. I seal my lips around the tube and blow steady and hard as if I'm inflating a balloon. The device beeps when it has enough air and Grimsdottir watches for the reading. After about twenty seconds she says with a curt smile,

"You have passed."

Grimsdottir tucks the breathalyser away inside her jacket and pulls out from another pocket a drug saliva kit. She opens the sealed packet and places the test tube on the roof. She then tears free from a clear plastic packet a short rod with a spongy swab at the end. I open my mouth in readiness.

"I swab for saliva, this takes a short time," she explains crisply.

She intrusively dabs and rubs for a period shorter than it feels. The rod is then screwed into the tube and a strip around the centre peeled off to reveal six spaced bands.

"We test for six drugs, it takes some minutes."

There is no idle talk, Grimsdottir makes notes and glances at the tube every so often. She finally inspects it with Sigurdsson looking over her shoulder and says,

"You are clear."

"Glad to hear it. Look there's damage to back of the car where we were rammed. They knocked us off the road and kidnapped Toni," I point out trying to steer the situation back on track.

I hold onto the side of the RAV and shuffle to the rear. Sigurdsson puts a hand out to stop me.

"I think you had better sit down Mr. Cutter."

I slump into the front passenger seat feeling dog-tired, and I hear myself mumbling the words,

"Do what you like, I'm past caring."

I close my eyes, wishing that I had just lied down and succumbed to the cold.

"Mr. Cutter are you all right?" says Sigurdsson.

"As good as someone can be who has been smacked around the head with a baseball bat, fallen off a cliff and is hypothermic," I complain sarcastically.

"The Rescue Team will be here in a few minutes and they have a medic," reassures Sigurdsson.

I exaggerate discomfort to buy time and close my eyes again. I hear them confer in Icelandic interspersed with occasional squawks from the radios. A few minutes elapse during which I am checked and roused by Sigurdsson. In between I attempt to corral my thoughts. Sigurdsson is working off bogus information supplied by? but like a gunshot spooking horses the pain scatters my thoughts decapitating any constructive thinking – I need direct answers.

I hear additional voices and turn in the seat flopping my feet out of the footwell onto the grass. Three men and a woman in bright red overalls with blue segments on the shoulders and knees traipse down the slope exchanging greetings with the police. There are now two four by four vehicles on the verge where the Defender had been. Both are white and have a blue emergency light rack, though one has jacked up tyres like a monster truck and has red livery instead of blue.

There is more talking that I am not privy to, which for a man prone to suspicion is an itch that cries to be scratched. One of the men carrying a heavy kit bag over his shoulder separates from the group and sits on his haunches in front of me. He is a strapping, young guy with a black bushy beard and shovels for hands.

"Hello, I am Kristofer and I am a medic from the Search and Rescue Team. I have been told that you have been hit in the head with a bat, and you have fallen some height. Is that correct?"

I nod my head, his English is superb, his accent mellifluous.

"How far did you fall?"

"About fifteen feet onto soggy grass."

"Good. What part of your body did you fall on?"

"My front I think. I don't remember."

"Did you lose consciousness?"

"Yes, I was stunned from getting hit by the bat, and I fell, then blacked out."

"Where do you hurt?"

"Head, I've a headache and I'm feeling very tired and dizzy some of the time."

He stretched a pair of latex gloves over his enormous hands and began to examine me. He looks into my ears for cranial leaking, feels for soft spots in my skull and checks my eyes with a pen light for non-reacting pupils.

"Do you feel pressure in your head?"

"No, just a headache."

"This is good. I don't think there is a problem, you may have a small concussion. I will give you some paracetamol for the pain. The cuts ... probably you don't need stitches," he says rocking his head side to side in indecision.

He produces a blister pack and a bottle of water from pockets in his kit bag and pops out two tablets. I take and swallow them with a gulp of water, and he gestures for me to keep the bottle.

Kristofer confers with Sigurdsson and I see Grimsdottir and the rest of the Search and Rescue Team trudge up the hill to the big wheeled SUV. They get into the raised cab and the vehicle trundles down the hill and towards the waterfall; the throaty engine and massive tyres making light work of the obstinate ground.

Sigurdsson seems like he is churning thoughts. To him this incident probably looks a lot like a spider diagram, at least that is how as a fellow stripey I would be looking at it in his position. At the centre there is what is alleged and branching out are the possibilities, lines of enquiry, procedures and evidence. In this case I would be working two spiders: one for the kidnap allegation and the other for the crock of shit car theft. The lines had to be followed and bottomed out: they led to dead ends, further lines of enquiry and conclusions. For instance, intoxicated driving was a possibility and had been tested and ruled out, however speeding or being rammed off the road are still viable explanations and had not been eliminated as a cause for the off-roaded RAV.

I wait for eye contact with Sigurdsson and then probe him for information,

"Sergeant Sigurdsson, Toni told me she rented this car, and she has been kidnapped; so, who is saying I stole it?"

"The person who it is hired to, Antonia Brookes. Mr. Cutter I'm going to have to ask you to accompany us to Borgarnes, so that we can investigate this report further; also, there is a hospital in Borgarnes we can take you to where you can be treated if you wish."

I understood the implication and didn't protest - it is better to cooperate than be arrested.

Antonia Brookes is that Toni's real name. Toni - An..toni..a; of course, it is just an abbreviation.

"Mr. Cutter, I'm going take some photographs of the scene and some will be of you to evidence how you look."

"They won't be flattering photographs then."

Sigurdsson grins,

"No, they won't."

He uses a small camera and takes around a dozen shots of the RAV and its path. He then asks me to stand and angling around me takes several more shots of my face, hands and person.

"Thank you Mr. Cutter I have enough now, you can sit back down."

The rescue vehicle returns, and Grimsdottir jumps out of the back seat. She is carrying a large clear plastic evidence bag with the baseball bat inside, the tip of the handle protruding from the top. She confers with Sigurdsson who stands wide with one arm across his belly, and the other propped upwards against it; the hand fidgeting with his chin and mouth.

The paracetamol is beginning to blunt the pain, and I'm feeling a little better from sipping the water which is now almost gone. Sigurdsson strides over and says with an open palm pointing to the verge,

"Okay Mr. Cutter we are leaving now I will carry your case. Do have any identification with you?

I unzip my travel bag and hand over my passport. He flicks through it and says,

"I'm going to keep this until we get to the police station. I will make a copy. I must also ask you for your safety and mine to empty your pockets."

I comply thinking that a search is something that I would have done from the get-go. I put my belongings on the bonnet of the RAV and lace my fingers around the back of my head in readiness for a frisk. Sigurdsson follows the cue and from behind methodically pats me over. He then has a cursory look at my things before saying,

"Okay you can keep these."

We trudge up the slope leaving Grimsdottir searching inside the RAV. Sigurdsson opens a rear door of the Nissan Pathfinder and I squeeze in behind a pushed back front driver's seat. Sigurdsson doesn't get in, instead he examines the road presumably for skid marks and collision debris. He takes some more snaps and uses the flash in the fading light. I watch him squat and pick up a large section of brake light casing and place it in an evidence bag. He strolls back to the police vehicle, and with phone in hand dawdles outside. A couple of minutes later Grimsdottir lugging a bag with my dirty clothes and looking a little out of puff appears. The cops exchange a few words, put the evidence bags and my case in the boot, and we set off for Borgarnes.

CHAPTER 11

The car is comfortable after Sigurdsson pulls the seat forward, and the warmth and motion soon send me to a welcome sleep. The car turns, and my head lolls to one side and I jerk awake.

We have entered a car park of a long two story white building with a brown sloped, corrugated roof that comes over the front like a fringe. The building is a modern design with indented windows. It resembles a set of three incomplete eights with a set back windowless block at the end. We slot into a space and my seized-up muscles ache as I get out. The day is closing, and the temperature has dropped, and I feel the chill breeze before going through the double doors of the station.

I'm led along a corridor to a toilet. Sigurdsson holds the door open and says,

"Perhaps you'd like to wash your face ... and use."

I badly need the urinal and I am there for nearly a minute. Following this I clean myself up the best I can in the wash basin. Then with dripping wet hair I am escorted further along the corridor to an interview room, which is plain, functional and windowless like they all are. It has a table with two chairs either side and on the table there is a double decked DVD recording device. Sigurdsson sits down and directs me to take a seat on the opposite side. I consider telling Sigurdsson I am Police Sergeant; it would probably help with my credibility; however, I have purposely left my warrant card at home. He could only count on my word for it unless he contacted my Force for verification, and I don't want them to have additional dirt to use on me. I decide to keep stumm and only pull it out of the bag if the situation continued to go sideways.

Grimsdottir brings in two Styrofoam cups of coffee and sets them on the table along with some packets of sugar and a plastic spoon. Sigurdsson leaves the sugar and hinging the cup between thumb and forefinger stands up. He blows into his coffee and I wait for him to speak, but he rocks on his heels and blows into his coffee. He finally takes a sip and says with a slow measured delivery,

"Thank you for helping us with our investigation. We have different stories and we need to find out which one is the truth. We are waiting for Antonia Brookes to come to the police station so we can ask her questions about the vehicle theft she reported."

I take a sip of coffee and pose a question I know the answer to,

"So, she didn't wait around for officers from where she made the report then?"

There is a pause and a reluctant,

"No."

"And she won't turn up here either, because she is in the boot of a car being taken to Isafjordur. You've bet on the wrong horse Sergeant," I remark in an authoritative tone.

Sigurdsson looks perplexed and I figure the idiom maybe lost on him. He responds,

"I am taking what you say seriously Mr. Cutter and there is evidence .... to back up your story. The police from the Western and Westfjord districts are looking out for the Land Rover. This is why you have not been arrested."

I sit back in the chair and relax. The bleach haired twat has succeeded in muddying the waters and dividing the police's attention - he must have forced her to make the call. It is a clever ruse creating a smokescreen for their escape, but when Antonia fails to show and her phone is off, the smoke will clear – no Toni equals no theft. I tap my Fitbit and the display reads 5:12 - they could have covered a lot of ground by this time.

My phone is on critical and I ask Sigurdsson if I can charge it. He agrees and I hook it up and I belatedly text Annabel to let her know I'm alright. I kill the minutes by reading the news and browsing a shooting forum I belong to. Sigurdsson is in and out of the room, and I frequently see him checking the chunky explorer type watch he wears. Time is the heel of a boot, incrementally crushing possibility – squashing the spider.

It is just after six o'clock when a plain clothes detective enters the room. In one hand he holds two coffees between splayed fingers and in the other a hard-backed A4 sized notebook. He sits down opposite me and precisely lowers the coffees to the table without any spillage. He is the wrong side of forty-five and has a haggard, bloated look to go with it. The split veins around his nose tell me he lives hard and is probably a closet drinker. He has neatly combed sandy coloured hair, is clean shaven and sports a smart, well-cut navy blue suit. A strong waft of quality aftershave could either mean he is serious about personal grooming, or that he is masking the stale stench of the previous night's binge.

The notebook has seen some use and he flips it open to near the end, lining it up parallel to the table's edge. A Parker pen is drawn from the handkerchief pocket of the jacket and is placed in the crease of the book, then a pair of stylish glasses are removed from an inside pocket and delicately put on. When he is done he places both palms on the table and in impeccable English introduces himself.

"I am Detective Gudjohnsen. I am here to further investigate the kidnapping of your female companion Antonia Brookes or Toni as you know her. I've been briefed that you met her for the first time last night at the Gaukurinn bar in Reykjavik, and that you have not had previous communications. I want you to start at the beginning; I will take notes and ask questions."

I relay the whole story and don't spare the details. At points Gudjohnsen interjects and I clarify or go over the segment of the story again. Certain questions I expand upon, others I do not know the answer to, and disappointingly I can't for the life of me remember the name of the old fella in Isafjordur. It is a key piece of information and I am embarrassed to have forgotten it. In the end I'm not sure what he makes of it all, but he has a platform to launch the investigation from: he has names, descriptions, a vehicle and a likely direction of travel.

Gudjohnsen puts his pen down for a moment and says,
"I'm going to type this up. At the back of the statement there are some fields I have to fill in. I have your personal details except your occupation."
Here goes,
"Police Sergeant."
Gudjohnsen nods and a minor warmth seems to come over an otherwise impassive exterior.
"When are you planning on returning home?"
"In a couple of days perhaps, in truth I don't really know the answer to that. It maybe earlier than my planned departure next Wednesday."
I mark Gudjohnsen as a fastidious man when he takes the same care and time reversing his desk routine. That type of man is thorough; however, this tends to come at the price of speed because they deliberate and fuss the fuck out of everything. He eventually stands up and says,
"I will contact you when the statement is ready, and you can sign it at the police station in Reykjavik City Centre."
I am relieved that I don't have to wait hours for this guy to painstakingly construct a statement. I lift myself off the chair feeling leaden and stiff as I follow Gudjohnsen out of the room. We stop at an office and he nips inside, returning with my passport, and a contact card. He hands me both and says sheepishly,
"If you need me or remember anything else I can be reached on that number. There is a bus going to Reykjavik that will be leaving soon and I will drive you to the bus stop. I would take you myself, but I have a lot to do. Your clothes and case are by the door."
I'm being hoofed out onto the street. I had hoped for a lift. I

guess kindness is in short supply for a fellow cop losing his way. I conceal my disappointment,
"No worries pal, you crack on."

It is an irritable night, starless and grubby black, beset by showers and an unkind wind. I huddle at the bus stop eating a hot sandwich counting the minutes until the bus arrives. I don't have to wait long and a yellow and blue bus pulls into the stop. The doors open with a hush and the driver confirms that the bus is going to Reykjavik. I snag and bang as I climb on board, desperately wanting to get back to the hotel, and for the wretched day to end. I pay two thousand two hundred Krona and would have paid anything he asked. There are plenty of seats, the tourists are in cars and coaches and I make myself comfortable.

I unzip a section of my case and slip in a hand. I grope around for the neck, and when found I tease it out. I turn from the aisle and slyly take a deep slug of whisky, my reflection a ghost in the window. The Glenlivet Nadurra pleasantly burns and I chug down more anticipating the warm embrace to come. I stare out of the window and the scenery drifts by, a distortion of darkened images, reflection and artificial light.

The Nadurra is pleasant company, though I'm not a snob, I'll associate with any of the harder boys and even the rough ones have their place at a push. Flick the switch Will and turn off. Don't go down the rabbit hole tonight. I double gulp and feel the reassuring burn in my belly. I take my own advice and conjure harmless thoughts, and if I slip I slug them away.

The bus pulls into Hlemmur Station and I clatter my way off. I check my phone and it is a six minute walk to the Storm. I um and ah about getting a taxi, the Scrooge in me wins and I force march to the hotel.

The receptionist cringes like Quasimodo has walked into the building. I am beyond caring and I just drag my stuff towards the lift. Inside the room I strip off, and for some minutes wallow in the shower cleansing myself of the dirt and blood. I dry off, take a final belt of whisky and sink into the bed.

I wake earlier than I would want and know there is no more sleep to be had. I crawl out of bed like an arthritic old man leaving a blotch of dried blood on the pillow. After freshening up and getting dressed I go downstairs and gorge on the breakfast buffet. I start with coffee, then make a thick cheese and ham sandwich with fresh cut bread. After that there is a plate of rollmops, boiled eggs, and baloney pate on crusty bread washed down with another coffee. Finally, I have a large helping of wonderful Danish pastries with a side order of berries, and a third coffee. I finish as most people are drifting in and wander over to the lounge where there is Wi Fi. I lower myself onto a soft sofa and let the breakfast settle.

I restlessly browse my phone with little interest, and occasionally look up at residents congregating in the foyer for excursions. I sit up, tap my foot and rub my hand across my mouth. I'm revisiting the car and our last moment together and I am bothered by it. There was a connection, a playful spark and a sexual sizzle that could have perhaps gone somewhere, and now is being thought of in the past tense. Alongside of that there is a profound sense of failing to discharge a duty, of abrogating a responsibility that had been assumed, of unfinished business and dashed pride. I have the need to search for her, so I enter tattooists in North Tonawanda into the search engine and three pop up. I dismiss the first called *Carl's Tattooing* and the second named *American Skin Art by Dead Ed* for obvious reasons. The third is called *Kraken Ink* on Main Street and I smile at the double meaning, knowing this is the one.

I click on the link to the website and see a photograph of her sitting at a work table wearing a black cut off t-shirt with her inked arms on show. She has on black latex gloves and is pushing a needle into a woman's back – this much is true then. I pinch a bit of my beard and twist it until there is a mild sensation of pain. I don't want to walk away, even though I know it to be a fool's errand to continue. I realize that not doing anything would plague me, and in doing something I would be kicking up a nest of vipers. What to do when between the devil and the deep blue sea?

Get Carter plays off the phone and it is a foreign number that I'm not going to answer. I listen to the music and imagine what Jack Carter would do. Jack would go north, he'd poke around until he got answers, then sort it out with a shotgun. Of course, in the end he is killed for his interference by a sniper's bullet he doesn't see - a bad augury then.

CHAPTER 12

I check the departure screen and it has changed to boarding. I hook my bag over my shoulder and make for the terminal, far from convinced that this is even remotely sane. It was a mad dash once the decision was made. I found a seat on a domestic flight to Isafjordur flying out out of Reykjavik City Airport at 12:15 and booked a taxi from the hotel to the airport immediately after.

It is an improbable looking aircraft. It is sleek bodied with comparatively stubby wings and a single propeller each side. On the white fuselage Flugfelag Islands is written in blue and there is a Pegasus emblem on the blue fin. I cross the tarmac with a small group of passengers and board the plane. I settle in my allocated seat and shortly after the safety brief the plane begins to taxi onto the runway. The take-off speed is slower than a jet-propelled plane, yet the take-off itself seems quicker and smoother.

We ascend to a cruising altitude and the pilot announces over the tannoy that it is a forty minute flight. I decide to use the time to formulate a plan of attack. I open a notepad application on my phone and write: SCHEME – something to do with Ron and the promise of money. The name doesn't ring true, although I don't have the right name to replace it – it is like trying to find a wisp of smoke in the mist. Of course, it could randomly come to me, or perhaps be revealed through an unseen connection, or then again not.

The facts I know and could deduce about Ron Somethingsson

are: he is or was into metal detecting and Viking history, is probably on account of his friendship with Toni's father aged between fifty-five and seventy-five, lives in Isafjordur and is currently being visited by a couple of unsavoury Americans. With a population of roughly two and a half thousand it is enough to go on, and I think I have a shot of finding him with some old fashion leg-work and door knocking. If not him, Marcus would stick out like a sore thumb, and there is also the Defender to look out for.

There is a spot of turbulence and the plane dips and rises and vibrates. I hear an involuntary gasp from someone in front, and in an opposite seat I see a young man look to the heavens and cross himself in prayer. I have tensed up without realizing and my breathing is shallow. I chastise myself for being a wuss and breathe out. I don't enjoy flying and used to be quite anxious with take-offs and landings. Over time I had improved but scrape the surface and the fear is still there. Beth used to say that I didn't like being out of control and that is true, because I hate the really big thrill rides at amusement parks as well. It made my story of being a firefighter ridiculous because I can't stand heights either.

The Pilot, in Icelandic and English reassures the passengers that the turbulence will pass and there is nothing to worry about. It lasts long enough for me to feel I'm going to see my breakfast again, but then subsides into a staccato rumbling that is more irritating than concerning. After a few minutes it ceases completely, and the pilot announces that we are approaching Isafjordur.

I peer out of the window and the plane descends over mountains into a horseshoe shaped inlet. The mountains are truncated and deeply wrinkled with vertical lines giving the overall appearance of a basin. Jutting out on the left side of the fjord is a scimitar shaped peninsula crowded with colourful, commercial buildings. The peninsula then clearing at the end to a dock. Snaking around the rim of the cobalt blue water is a road. Attached to this at the back of the fjord there is a round shaped cluster of road connected buildings, set in a treeless greenery of shrub and grass.

The pilot tracks the road as it skirts around the mountain and banks right; and in a short distance the runway is visible. It is rudimentary: a thick strip of white lined road laid upon a larger section of light grey concrete, which in turn is constructed upon a spit of land in the water. The airport is three buildings and a fire truck with a short track joining at ninety degrees with the main road.

The dramatic mountains, rugged terrain and sparseness of population conjure in my in mind a romantic notion of entering a wild frontier town - even if in reality it couldn't be more civilized with its museums, mud soccer and music festivals.

We touch down and taxi around to the control tower. I grab my bag and file off the plane and the cold stings like a slap in the face. I nuzzle into my coat and follow the other passengers to the terminal. Having left my case at the Storm I leave the others to wait for their luggage and head outside. Next to the door I stop at a display of flyers and leaflets advertising what Isafjordur has to offer the tourist. A couple take my interest: The Westfjords Heritage Museum and The Osvor Maritime Museum. I slip the leaflets in my pocket and continue outside.

There are several taxis waiting and I make eye contact with the driver of the first in line. He is a middle-aged man with unruly grey hair and a down-turned mouth that made him look displeased with his lot. He is driving a white Kia saloon and I jump in the front. I tell him that I want to go to the Heritage Museum, and he drops his head, which I infer as a sign of agreement. He spins the car around and we cruise along the coastal road. The radio plays an Icelandic folk song while the driver puffs away on an e-cigarette - the vapour like honey and almonds. Gazing out from all the windows I suck in the stunning landscape like a drowning man would air – it is truly a remarkable place to live.

The taxi travels at a sedate pace to the other side of the fjord. Then into the peninsula to where it fattens out into dockyard warehouses and a patch of waste ground behind. The driver pulls in front of a low, brown wood building with a disproportionately high black roof, that is one of four historic buildings from another century. It flies a blue flag from a flagpole fixed to the left apex and has a windowed cupola in the centre of the roof line. If not for the skylight roof it would resemble a cabin from the wild west. I pay the fare but don't extend to a tip - that down-turned mouth can stay that way.

The entrance is a long wooden gangplank leading to an open double doorway of darkness and dim light. On washed grey pebbles to the right is an A frame made of weathered logs, that by the rusted hooks dangling from the centre pole would have hung chunks of meat and fish to be cured. I have a hunch that this could be a good place to start enquiries. I shell out the admission fee with a tinge of resentment at how much money is flying out of my hands. Beth had been careful with money and over the years it had rubbed off on me. It is funny and inevitable how people in long, happy relationships blended their characters.

There are no surprises inside. The interior is as you would expect it to be from the outside - pared down to bare utility. There are a party of tourists milling around the exhibits busy clicking away with cameras and smartphones. An overly made up young woman with a duck's bill for a top lip and fake lashes that could bat a fly, strikes a provocative pose next to an old fisherman's oilskin. She pouts glossed lips and sticks out her ass like it were a shelf for a drink. She manoeuvres the selfie-stick into position and gurns her way through several shots.

I'm fascinated by the rampant vanity and how some young women are turning themselves into freaks with filler and Botox – and how the men are following suit. I stop short of gawping at the incongruity of old and new and move under a low ceiling propped up by heavy wood struts. The ground floor is dedicated to the fishing industry. There are many grainy black and white photographs of fishing trawlers and fishermen's wives gutting fish, along with compasses, model ships, a whaling harpoon and an old brass porthole helmet diving suit with weighted shoes.

There is a guide in what I assume is traditional female dress for the region. She is a large lady in a full black swishy dress that reaches the ankles, with a plaid pinafore worn over the top and adorned with a huge bow on her chest. She is busy giving a talk to a group of tourists, so I leave her alone. I look for another guide and there isn't one. I see a steep wooden staircase and climb it hoping to find someone to speak to. There are fewer people wandering around the exhibits of regional flora and fauna and I find a tour guide. She is slighter and older and dressed the same, except I now notice that the traditional dress includes a black woollen skullcap. The tag on her chest informs me her name is Agatha.

On the ride over I had contemplated how best to go about it, and whichever way it was phrased I sounded like an idiot with only half of an idea of what I was talking about. I stand in front of her and wing it,

"Hi, I wonder if you can help me?"

"I will if I can," she replies, the small features of her face posing in anticipation.

"I'm looking for a local man who is into Viking history and metal detecting. I guess he would be around fifty-five to seventy-five years of age. I think his name is ... Ron or something similar," I say waveringly and with a hint of embarrassment. I smile awkwardly like you do when you wing something, and you don't expect it to turn out well.

"Perhaps you mean Jon, he volunteers here."

It strikes me like a lightning bolt, and I leap at it,

"Yes, Jon."

"Why are you looking for him?" her dainty features crinkling with suspicion.

I scramble into prevarication and reach for an answer.

"Because ... because I read about him on Trip Advisor, but can't remember his name, the ... the reviews said he was a great guide. My mistake I got mixed up ... Osvor, Maritime, Heritage."

I tapped my head and goofed like a fool.

She nods, and a lightness returns to her face,

"Yes, Jon Einarsson is very good, but he is not working today.

The Heritage and Maritime are the same. We get this all the time but the Osvor is separate and just outside of town."

I've painted myself into a corner with this gal, but at least I now have the right name.

"Thank you, you've been a great help," and as I say this I can almost hear her mind ticking as it doubles back on itself.

I turn and make for the stairs before what I told her doesn't add up - it didn't to me.

Outside the sky is a dirty, sunless white already signalling surrender to the coming darkness. I lean against the bow of a grounded rowing boat and ponder my next move. I must convince a local to tell me where he lives. I also have to think about where I will stay the night. I return to the museum entrance and loiter at the door. The cashier is wrapped up speaking with a girl and I bide my time until the girl's parents call her way.

"Excuse me I wonder if you can help me. I am supposed to be meeting Jon Einarsson at two o'clock and he is not here. I would message him, but I lost my phone in the sea when I tripped and banged my head whale watching. We've been emailing and messaging each other for a couple of months, and he offered to put me up for the night. Could you tell me where he lives, I'm going to be stuck otherwise?"

The cashier is a young bespectacled man with a leaf size wine birthmark on the side of his neck. He opens his mouth to speak but does not say anything. I can tell that he knows but doesn't know what to say so I labour the point some more. I try to look harmless and pathetic by huffing and shrugging and smiling inanely like I am too stupid to be a danger. I say despondently,

"I really am going to be stuck if I can't find Jon."

The cashier lifts his eyes as if the right answer has come to him and says,

"What is your name, I'll phone him and tell him that you're here."

I groan inwardly,

"My name is Will."

The cashier pulls a gold iPhone from his back pocket and swipes and taps the screen. He puts the phone to his right ear, and I can just about hear the ringing. The cashier smiles as the phone rings close to a dozen times without answer.

"He's not answering," says the Cashier shaking his head and opening his mouth again like a contemplative goldfish. Finally, he says,

"I would like to help but unfortunately I can't give out employee details."

I nod understandingly and take a step out the door before thinking of another tack.

"I understand you can't tell me where Jon lives, but is there somewhere in town that I might find him?"

The cashier protrudes his bottom lip and says,

"Yes ... you might see him at Bakarinn. It is a café in Hafnarstraeti. He likes the American woman there."

I take heart. I just got to fire enough shots off and I'll eventually hit the target. I ache like I'm ill and I push on into town wanting something to loosen me up. The phone does the headwork and I follow the track on the map to Bakarinn. The town is spacious like they have more space than they know what to do with; and bright, nearly all the hotels and houses are an uplifting white, blue, yellow or red. Back home the houses are packed and stacked into terraces for the working class and increasingly the underclass. Space matters so there isn't any, and in the dingy, choked streets the town closes in to stifle the life out of you.

I am now partially guilty of a modern ill by referencing my phone while walking, and as I look back up I catch the tail end of a petrol blue SUV rolling by. I hastily read the back and it is a Land Rover Defender. It rounds a corner and I make out at least three heavily clothed occupants that I can't even tell are man or woman. Instinctively, I go after it like a whippet bolts for a rabbit, though at the moment all my old beat up body can manage is a spirited jog.

Their Defender is green, or is it? It had been a dark, dismal day with a thrashing downpour and in such conditions a dark blue could easily be perceived as a dark green – I had to allow for error.

Clearing the corner, I see it at about a hundred yards distance turn again. I huff; pissed off from the spurred exertion. My boots pound the pavement and the sour remnants of last night's whisky surface. I am ragged by the time I reach the second corner, the deep, hard breaths rasping my lungs – I am not in the shape I was. Living with the black dog and the wages of whisky, the lethargy of the office, they had all taken their toll on my fitness.

I direct my eyes to the furthest point of a long street and the Defender is not to be seen. I stride purposely overtaking and side stepping the leisurely Sunday afternoon crowd, scouring back along lines of parked cars and junctions to side streets. In the third side street I see it parked up. Uneasily I approach, my senses all over it scratching for information. It is outside a restaurant and no longer occupied. I pull up the hood of my coat and walk past, furtively inspecting the front for damage. Everything is intact, however there are cattle bars and with those there to protect the front there might not be any. I try and think if the Defender had cattle bars and I don't remember either way.

I turn and withdraw into an adjacent doorway of a shut store where my brain works overtime. Marcus and Adam couldn't take Toni in for a casual meal. Perhaps at knife point it is possible, but too risky even for a psychopath; though there is always a question mark over what the mentally unhinged will or will not do. I had learned the hard way not to apply your own values to this calculation because for some people two plus two equals five. I stand shrouded in the doorway with wisps of steamy sweat curling out of my hood, mulling over at least half a dozen possibilities. Toni could be trussed up and gagged in the boot, but if that is the case who is the third person – Jon, an unknown accomplice. The other explanation that I had been too carried away with to yet consider is probably the most plausible, that it is a different Defender with different people. Yet, this is an uncommon vehicle in a very small town and in the destination where they were heading. The pendulum swings back and I must rule it out.

The restaurant is on the ground floor of a beige four story building, that has a peculiar tilted green roof like a cocked hat. It has numerous windows and square wooden pillars supporting a canopy along a glass frontage spanning two sides of the building.

From what I can deduce Hamraborg is a burger joint loosely modelled on an American diner. I walk to the door and abort entering when I realize that I don't have to go in to survey those inside. The two sided front means I can look fully into the restaurant.

I start at one corner and walking slowly scan the customers. I draw an apprehensive look off an old man seated drinking coffee when I get up onto the balls of my feet to peer beyond him. I methodically head hunt along the rows of booths eliminating everyone I fix my eyes on. I am near completion when I see two women and a man in their early twenties sitting at a booth. The woman unwinds a scarf and a man across from her shrugs off his coat. The third places a glove on top of another on the edge of the table – they look like they've just sat down, and I peg them for the Land Rover. There are two more booths: one is empty and the other is filled by a family. I puff out through my lips and then grin. I'd struck out, but never mind it was worth a shot, there was no other way to know.

My map re-routes and in little over a minute I reach a three storey oat coloured building, which has businesses on the ground floor and apartments or offices above. The Bakarinn Café is on the end with a light blue sign above high windows. I hold the door for two women leaving and go in. There is an attractive woman aged around fifty behind the counter. She has braided blonde hair with streaks of red, and a voluptuous figure straining against a fluffy Icelandic cardigan. She is looking down, reading a book through a pair of snazzy glasses.

"Hello," I say cheerfully.

"Hello, what can I get you honey?" she answers in an unmistakable southern drawl.

"I'd like a strong milky coffee and a salmon bagel with cream cheese thank you."

"Okay sweetheart, that's fifteen hundred Krona."

I fork out the money still unsure of what coins are worth.

"Take a load off sugar, and I'll bring it right over."

She has the confident ease and sassiness of a woman that has dealt with countless numbers of people from all walks of life. I imagine her to be a worldly veteran of bars, casinos and diners with a trunk load of hard luck stories and heartbreak. What I wonder had caused her to up sticks and set up shop at the edge of the world? A more pertinent question is what am I doing here? I have reasons though I don't know if I trust them. If I'm honest, I don't know right now if I trust myself at all.

"There you go darlin, enjoy!"

"Hey doll, could I ask you something?"

I never spoke like this, it just came out, and sort of felt appropriate.

"Sure hun."

"Do you know Jon Einarsson? I was supposed to meet him this afternoon at the museum where he volunteers, and he hasn't shown up. I'd phone him but I lost it overboard yesterday whale watching in Reykjavik. Trying to get a better angle on a shot, slipped hit my nut and over it went. Can you believe it?" I laugh self-deprecatingly and point to the prop of my most recent lies. "Could you tell me where he lives? I'm meant to be staying with him."

I am useless with women; however, I try to swing it with my best puppy dog look.

"I was expecting him myself today for lunch, but he didn't show. You is friend or something?"

I had heard and liked this accent on numerous films and television shows, and it is even richer and sexier in person.

"Yeah, even though I've never met him I'd say we were friends. We are both into Viking history and I met him on an internet forum a year ago. We chat regularly and when I said I was going to tour Iceland he invited me to Isafjordur to stay with him."

I may not like lying, even as it turns out I am not too shabby at it. It seems the more you do the slicker you get.

"Jon lives at twenty-two Hildevargur, it is sign posted and just off the hook. Tell him Nula don't like being stood up."

Nula jots it down on a napkin, and then sways her hips back behind the counter. I knew what she meant by hook, and remembering my lie in time, withdraw an empty hand from my coat pocket where my phone is. I tuck into the bagel and coffee and leave with a new found spring in my step.

CHAPTER 13

It is a small town, and everything isn't far, and Hildevargur is a stone's throw from the café. It is a quiet residential street and I don't see the Defender parked up anywhere, though my heart still beats for a fight. I had just crossed the street when my phone rings. I answer,

"Hello."

"Is that Mr. Cutter?" the voice formal and Icelandic.

"Yes it is," I reply thinking it is Gudjohnsen over Sigurdsson though I wouldn't bet money on it.

"It is Detective Gudjohnsen. How are you today?"

"Better than I was yesterday thank you for asking."

"Good," he said stiffly. "I've completed your statement and informed the Desk Sergeant that you will be in to sign it."

"Yeah no problem I'll call in."

"We haven't found Miss Brookes yet, but I'd thought you might want to know that we did find what we believe to be a burnt out Land Rover Defender near Staour."

"Is that near Isafjordur?"

"No, but on the way."

So, they had acted smart and ditched the Defender. They would still need wheels though and must have hired or stolen another vehicle. Now one of the things I am looking out for had gone. I would have to rely on the other two. It is a setback, but there are usually setbacks, a smooth ride is a rarity.

Number twenty-two is a reasonably large white house with green frame windows and door. It is set in a lush garden of leafy trees and bushes that have upon them the yellow wan of Autumn.

I step forward with trepidation; a familiar sense of dread of discovering death or the wanted in the next room, hanging from the attic or crammed in the wardrobe. I carefully climb the garden steps like they are creaky stairs and it is four o'clock in the morning. I'm assuming the worst that Jon is gone, or in a pool of blood behind the door.

The curtains are drawn, and I slink around the side of the house, pausing each step to sense for disturbance. I drop to a crouch and peer around the corner to the back. There is a shed close to a border fence and leaning against the shadowed side is a spade. The spade feels like Christmas has come early and I sidle over to fetch it. It is light, flat and narrow bladed, and a hard jab with it will split a nose in two. If I get into it with Marcus again I'm going to have to fight smarter to my advantages and not his, though I guess it will depend on where we fight and with what. I shove thoughts of revenge to the back of my mind and concentrate on the task in hand.

The blinds are drawn on the back windows, so I have no idea of what is inside. I creep to the side of the back door and listen intently and don't hear anything. I examine the door, it is wood on the bottom and textured glass above and it is shut. There is no blind, though only indistinct shapes and shades of light can be made out. I almost miss it, a small split in the frame level with the lock exposing untreated wood. I look closer and see prize marks in the join of the door, that caused the frame to split and perhaps the door to be breached.

I run through my options: I could wait outside for an opportunity to ambush, though that had too many variables - foremost being they could have already flown the coop. I could involve the police, but this meant relinquishing control of the situation, and that is drawing a sword that can cut both ways. The third option is the one I know in my gut I'm going to go for.

I gather myself, spade at the ready and test the door handle with a gloved hand. The lock is bust, and it gives. I step back and nudge the door wide open with the spade. I angle left and right round the doorway spying into the corners. The door has swung right and I'm happy that left is clear. I position myself on the doorstep, and side step in with the spade held as a bayonet to face what might be behind the door. There is nobody; a cluttered open plan kitchen leading to a worn lounge, both with several potted plants of various sizes. There is a pile of dried washing on a dining table, a cat bowl on a mat, papers on a coffee table, an analogue clock that ticks loudly. It is a little untidy though not disturbed.

Behind me there is a door and I pull it open like a poised Spartan, to find a damp laundry room with mouldy corners and flaking paint. I move through the kitchen into the lounge where on the left I see an open doorway to the hall. The floor is weathered block wood, with a sheepskin rug rumpled against the staircase featured on the opposing wall. The front door is to my right, another open doorway into a room of unknown purpose is directly opposite. Set in the side of the staircase is a closed door.

I step through and knock the handle of the spade against the frame of the door. The sound amplifies in the hallway and I may as well have rapped the front door like l am delivering a parcel. I curse with my lips that I'm a bungling fucking idiot and drop any further pretence at stealth. I storm through the open doorway ready for mayhem into a library of musty books and wall hung artefacts. As soon as I am in I am out and up the stairs, bounding, senses overloaded, everything at full throttle. I tear through the upstairs rooms with the commitment of a Kamikaze, but death or glory do not befall me. The rooms are absent except for the lingering presence of an old man living on his own.

Down the stairs at a gallop to the door underneath. It is a cupboard or basement and I hope it is a cupboard. I open the door and to the right stairs descend into darkness. There is a light cord and I pull it. Light floods the stairway holding the black unknown at bay. The stairs creak, give and feel treacherous and I hold onto the rail. Time has now slowed, and the blaze of adrenaline has quelled to sickness. They weren't here, though what they might have disposed of could be. I reach the bottom, the air is stuffy and clinging, the darkness overbearing the pocket of light. There is a tarnished metal light switch on the wall, and I move a hand towards it.

Suddenly I hear a murmur from the dark depths of the room. I recoil against the wall bracing the spade like a frightened peasant with a pitchfork. No terror emerges from the darkness, though the murmur persists, and I discern it is mechanical – a monotonous humming whirr. I breathe again and hit the switch.

◆ ◆ ◆

She is taped to a chair. Shiny grey Duct tape wound around the seat and her thighs, wrapped around her calves and the legs of the chair. Lengths and lengths of tape binding her body and arms to the back of the chair. There is a strip across her mouth and another over the eyes. Her head is slumped into her chest and it is not clear if she is alive or dead. I drop the spade and rush over to her. I say breathily,

"Toni, it's okay it's me Will."

She raises her head and the fear loosens its grip. I shed my gloves and peel back the tape from her eyes and mouth. The fan heater in the corner blows out heat and I feel the sudden break of sweat on my forehead. She looks shocked to see me - shocked full stop.

"Are you hurt?" I ask.

"Banged up a bit and hot as hell. Fuck! You came for me. I saw you fall. I thought you were dead."

"There's time for that yet," I joke.

I begin ripping away the tape, stopping halfway to kill the heater. I bite, peel and pull and soon Toni is free. I help her up and we climb out of the basement.

In the kitchen Toni takes off her brown leather flight jacket with a sheepskin collar and lapels and pulls up the red micro-fleece underneath. On her stomach a purple black bruise resembling a disfigured flower stands out against the whiteness of her skin.

"I bet there is a bigger one on my leg; the fucker kicked me like a dog."

"He showed me he knows how to use a bat, and he looks to me like he's done a fair bit of karate."

"He has, he's been state champion a couple of times. His father ran a dojo in Rochester and started instructing him from the age of four," she says begrudgingly.

I would adapt. I did it all the time on the street deploying the right tactics for the job. I realized his is a speed game that relied on space and movement. If I could shut that down, get it close and dirty I would murder him. I feel a spark of excitement as I visualize the edge, car, corner I would smother him in.

I put my gloves back on and close the back door, then from the kitchen tap I pour two tall glasses of water. Toni chugs hers down, droplets of water spilling from the sides of the glass and rolling off her chin. She goes for a refill, finishes half of it and breathes heavily. She wipes her mouth dry and wearily says,

"I am going to tell you the truth, I owe you that."

"I'd be glad to hear it," I reply.

"You remember what I told you about my dad being stationed over here with the Navy?"

"Yeah."

"Like I said in his spare time he used to roam the island treasure hunting with a metal detector. Well he thought he never really found anything of consequence or value ... but he had he just didn't know it. It was Jon who found out what he had. Jon has devoted his life to Icelandic history: the first settlers, the sagas, the lore and legends. Early last year Jon was researching the legend of Gorm Longbeard's hidden treasure and he found an obscure reference to a key."

"Right!"

I draw out the word feeling my credulity being stretched - Gorm Longbeard sounded like a Tolkien dwarf; however, crimes were being committed for something, so I knocked it off and listened. Toni shot me a cut it out look, and continued,

"This Viking wore an ornate brooch on his cloak and Jon believes the design of it is a map. Jon is convinced my father's broach is Longbeard's brooch. The filaments in the centre replicate a feature of land and Jon thinks he has found what it represents. Jon says that the brooch has to be looked through at the correct distance and the lines matched up. When it is aligned the cross in the south east corner is where the treasure is buried."

"X marks the spot," I playfully contribute.

It was all very fanciful and farfetched. I hadn't met Jon Einarsson, however my policeman's mind already wanted to label him an eccentric quack. He might have something, but years of listening to people who believed they were tracking UFOs, had their bedsits bugged by the government or possessed mystical powers had warped my perspective. Now I had to drag the dial back to the centre to create an open mind.

Toni pulls out a chair from underneath the kitchen table and sits down. I lean back against the sink keen to hear more.

"Initially Jon spoke to my father, wanting him to fly over so that they could find it together. However, my father is dying with lung cancer and is too ill to travel. My father told me about it and told Jon to talk to me. Jon and I discussed an expedition to locate Gorm's Gold. It took awhile to save the cash for the trip. I had been seeing Marcus for a couple of years and he always had his nose in my business, badgering me about this or that, snooping around my affairs. I told him before he found out and his face lit up like Las Vegas at night. He was all in whether I liked it or not. He made up the shortfall in cash and had all these plans with what he was going to do with the money. We were set to book when we had a massive bust up, one of many horrific rows that always ended with him hurting me. I left him and booked my own trip. It is my father's legacy not a bankroll for his coke deals."

In a bizarre way it made sense like finishing a jigsaw puzzle of a surrealist painting. The pieces fitted even if you weren't sure of the picture. It isn't much of a revelation that Marcus is mixed up in coke, but to what extent is Toni tarred by that brush? Perhaps more than I'd want to think. I fill in the rest.

"He followed you here with his sidekick. He trawled the bars and found you. He attacked you in the alley to get the brooch."

Toni nodded then added,

"He was tracking my phone from an app he secretly installed. He's been gloating about it, telling me what a dumb bitch I am. And you know what, he's right I am stupid, I should have never got involved with him. My friend Cynthia warned me I was playing with fire."

I could see how tired she is carrying this monkey on her back. Men like him wore women down like sandpaper until they had no self-worth. Until they didn't even know who they were anymore.

"He now has what he needs, he has got the brooch and he's taken Jon," Toni concludes. "Once I led them here they didn't need me any longer. I know they thought about killing me."

"You're a loose end. And as the stakes get higher there is a tipping point where snipping the loose end makes sense. Jon is also a problem and I don't see how this works out for anyone now."

I then thought of a question and it came about the same way as finding a small stone in your shoe – a gradual, uncomfortable realization.

"If you and Jon had met up and found the treasure. Treasure of historical value. What would you have done with it?" I ask loading the gun.

Toni shifts in the seat, rakes a hand through her hair and looks me dead in the eye. She answers in a casual, offhand way,

"I don't know. Smuggle it to the states in a fishing boat I suppose and trade it on the antiquities black market. If the legend is true Jon reckons we could be talking a million five, or even two with the right buyer."

Toni then frowned into an expression of someone discovering that their dog had dumped all over the hallway mat.

"Or we could dig it up and hand it over to the government

who'll put it into a museum and charge folks to see it. I don't know about you, but I think that belief and hard work deserve reward."

And she looks through her brow and bites her bottom lip like she is aiming a rifle, and I am the target.

I have entered a quandary. In Britain found treasure had to be declared and I do not think it would be any different in Iceland. It would be a crime to keep it and another to illicitly sell it on the black market. On the other hand, it is a victimless crime, especially as the government doesn't even know it exists. It would simply be depriving the Icelandic people of something they don't know they have. It is the spoils of Viking pillage buried in the ground for a thousand years, so you could even argue it doesn't even belong to them in the first place. Shouldn't the people who made the sacrifices to find it reap the rewards? I know what side of this argument I should be on yet I'm not on it – I'm impaled on the fence.

Toni reads me like a billboard and glides over. She clasps my hand and caresses it with her thumb. She combs her fingers through the back of my hair and kisses me softly on the lips. Then more ardently and my stomach dips. She pushes her mouth onto mine, invading with her tongue, sensuously assaulting my lips with her teeth. I am overrun and reason has routed. She lets go of me and I draw breath.

"I like you Will. I did the moment I laid eyes on you. And the more I learn of your character the more I get to like you. We have something Will, you wouldn't be here if you didn't feel it."

"I know ... yes you're right," I feebly mouth.

The best things often had no rhyme or reason, they thrived beyond the rational.

"I overheard them I know where they have gone. We can follow them, free Jon and get the brooch back."

"As easy as that. Breeze over, point out to them the error of their ways and ask for it back. If we carry on with this there is no way it ends without bloodshed," I reply flatly.

"Perhaps there is a way ... we could steal it back."

"How ... how are we going to steal it back? It's not like he's going to keep it in the car overnight or leave in a changing room while taking a leisurely swim is it?" I retort with a heavy dose of sarcasm.

"It is a lot of money and I can't stand the thought of that prick getting his hands on it."

There is venom in her voice.

"And what he did to me and what he done to you, and what he's done to others ... he needs to pay. It is right that he pays for the shit that he's done. I've seen him kick a poor, hapless kid full out in the head for no other reason than to see him hit the ground ... he's a complete cunt! and something bad needs to happen to him."

Her voice still venomous quivers with emotion and a tear comes to her eye.

"If you help me to get it we'll split it three ways. That'll be at least five hundred k for your retirement fund."

Money didn't get my juices flowing. I had enough for my needs and never sought more than that. I could find ten thousand pounds in a drug search and ten thousand pounds would be handed in. It is other things that drive and irk me. But what if I didn't go back to the emasculating drudgery of the office? If I no longer wore stripes to tell me who I am. If no longer boxed in and owned by the company – what then? A chasm of possibility opened up like a boat unhitched from its moorings and pulled by uncertain currents out into the wide sea. I should go for it, because it is better to be dashed on the rocks than to rot in the harbour.

"Fuck it I'm in. We'll talk splits later, let's find it first."

Toni flings her arms around my neck and kisses me hard. With a glint in her eye she says,

"After this we'll be unbreakable."

CHAPTER 14

Toni has the idea to look for car keys. I peer around the blind of the lounge window and see that there is a white Ford Ranger parked outside. The keys aren't in the usual places on key hooks or tables by either outside door. Whilst looking I find a plastic bag and I go back into the basement to pick up all the tape that will have my fingerprints and saliva all over it. I also pick up the spade because it feels good in my hands given the work ahead. In the study behind a mahogany desk is an alcove with a metal detector resting upright. I take it and continue the search.

I am in the hallway when I hear a clank from close outside. It sounds like someone walking over a metal drainage cover like the one I had avoided creeping around the house. Toni is in the lounge lifting a magazine on the coffee table.

"Toni!" I hush putting a finger over my lips.

She pricks up like a nervous rabbit and I call her over. I pull her into the study, and I press myself against the side of the doorway with the spade ready to fire. I glance over my shoulder and Toni is releasing a Viking hand axe from a mount on the wall.

The thought that It could be the police crosses my mind, and if it is I will put the spade down and take what is coming to me. I hear the back door open without a knock – could it be Jon, would they have released him so soon? I open my mouth to call out and stifle the sound. I hear the clump of footsteps on block flooring, and then a voice that I kind of recognise projecting malevolence through the house.

"Don't get your hopes up slut! I'm the last man you're ever going to see."

I peel away from the wall and burst through the doorway into the hall – it is clear. I break right towards the basement door and it is open and glowing with a shadowy light. Into the mouth I steer the spade bending with the tight turn down into the stairway. Three quarters the way up turned on the stairs is Adam. His scalp glistens with sweat, his black bruised eyes ghoulish, the mouth snarled and fevered like a rapist. A large, thin bladed filleting knife gleams in his hand, the spade like a spear in mine and there is a brief moment of knowing that is shattered by violence.

I stab and beat downward at the would be killer and he fends frantically with his free hand. He bulls forward trying to grab the spade while reaching upwards with frenzied knife strokes and desperate cries. A thrust of the spade splits his forearm to the bone and another gouges a chunk of flesh from his skull. I gather a grim momentum and he bows from a flat, thunking blow to the top of the head. I chop the spade down again, but he shifts to his right and the left side of the blade awkwardly clips his shoulder, twisting and loosening in my hands. I recover my grip and set to strike, yet before I do he lunges and stabs me in the left shin. It feels like a punch though I know I've been stabbed, and I am surprised that there is no sharp pain. He withdraws the knife and stabs, snagging and slicing the outer flesh of my calf.

Before I am stabbed further I hook the spade upward and across cracking him hard underneath the chin. He jerks up, thudding against the hand rail sliding backwards along it, turning, pitching headlong down the stairs. He rolls, limp limbs flailing, the body bending over itself, the head folding and smacking the wooden steps that are as bare and harsh as the teeth of a saw. Adam hits the bottom curled like a fat cat in the sun, his head angled against the wall, the knife skewered through both cheeks.

Standing looking down at the bleeding sorry mess I am responsible for I am overcome with nausea and have to hold onto the rail.

"Do you think he's dead?" Toni says.

"I fucking hope not. Dead is a real fucking problem," I sigh.

In a consequence free world, I would have no remorse for what I'd done - Adam got what he deserved. The sickness is selfish. I had dug a great big hole for myself and now the earth is being shovelled in. I turn to see Toni behind me on the top step with the short war axe held at the ready in both hands.

"I think he meant to kill you with that knife," I say.

"Yeah that's my feeling too, I guess they had a rethink about loose ends. Wait ... Marcus, where is Marcus?"

My body sinks like it is loaded with weight and I don't know if I can face another round. I climb the stairs after Toni, my shin squeezing out pain with each step.

My brain is jammed with possibilities, and in the lounge I twist in indecision. Adam is done; hopefully not deceased but with that bone crunching tumble he had to be out of play. I reassure myself that I am not going to get a knife in the back and that I only needed to be concerned with Marcus. Toni and I exchange anxious looks before taking up ambush positions either side of the back door. I nervously shift and alter stance and my shin stings with each adjustment; blood welling in my boot.

I make eye contact with Toni and point to the axe. I shake my head and wave it off. I point to the spade and nod and she shrugs a reluctant agreement – there is no way back from an axe in the head, though we may already be too far down the road for it to matter. The seconds stretch out interminably and I grow impatient. I scowl and fidget until the tension swells beyond what I can endure. I don't know and the need to know is killing me. The house feels like a trap about to be sprung and I want out of it.

I slip out the back door into the cold darkness and manoeuvre around the slabbed path. Branches rustle in the wind revealing and concealing multicoloured spots of light from the street and peninsula below. I get to the front and a strong gust sways the trees to a whooshing crescendo as I see the profile of a woman. She is sitting in the driver's seat of a dark coloured SUV, her face lit by the screen glow of the phone she is viewing. She is dark skinned and striking with curly black hair sprouting out the sides of a grey woollen Beanie hat.

There is someone next to her in the passenger seat, but I can't make out any more than that. The SUV is parked up next to the Ranger.

I move briskly down the garden path and on closer inspection the SUV becomes a gunmetal Mitsubishi Warrior. The situation throws me, and I slow my step. I become conscious of my menacing silhouette, and the fear I could cause this poor unsuspecting woman, if she is here for an innocent reason.

The woman looks up in my direction and a moment later a powerful side roof light shines dazzlingly into my eyes. I hear the rev of an engine and a screech of tyres, and the beam sweeps several gardens as the Warrior barrels down the street. I curse my policeman's hesitancy, the need to measure, balance and justify action that always put you a split second behind the criminal. The criminal who simply acted as he needed to – shooting first and asking questions later.

"Did you see the woman?" I ask.

"Yeah."

"Who is she?"

"I've no idea. Look we'd better find those keys and get out of here, she might phone the cops again."

The thought struck a febrile dread and I could feel the choke on time – there would be minutes before the noose pulled tight.

"Look for the keys and I'll deal with Adam."

"What are you going to do?"

She poses with a hint of dare, her penetrating, sky blue eyes scouring me for a read of intention.

"I'm not sure."

"Whichever," she replies with solemnity.

"I'm with you either way."

We go back inside, Toni riffles the draws and I brood my way to the basement. At the top of the stairs I look down. Adam is sitting upright in the corner, his legs splayed in front of him, his back arching and curving through waves of agony. His right hand quivers next to the knife still embedded in his cheek; and a phone out on his lap vibrates with a muffled ring.

I descend the stairs, my boots resonating on the timber like a death knell. Adam rolls his head in my direction; his eyes enlarge as though they are trying to eject from his head. He emits a gurgled whimper and rips the knife out of his cheek, and in the confined space I am deafened by the choking scream. I know if our roles were reversed I would die in a frenzy of stabs and slashes; and if he had time, that is what I would probably get – a prolonged death. I would put down money that given the chance he'd torture – after all the twisted prick had hung a dog.

I stop five steps up from him and assess the damage: he is spluttering blood though this is probably the pierced cheeks and will cease in time. The gouge to the head is congealing, the jaw is misshapen and is almost certainly broken. The flat blow to the top of the head is unlikely to have fractured the skull, though the fall could have. He appears to have injured his back and I can see a bone protruding from his left forearm. If he hasn't internal bleeding then he'll live - well probably.

He holds the knife out like a crucifix. I show him the spade and he flinches.

"No please, mother of god no more," he begs pitifully.

"You're on your own. Your buddy and the girl have left you with me." I state with a cold finality.

I let the thought take hold before continuing,

"You're done, it's over for you," and I use the spade as a pointing stick to cast over his body where it has split and broke.

"Every time we meet Adam, you get hurt, and I'll happily hurt you some more if you don't do as I say."

I loom over him with the spade and he shrinks into the corner engulfed by my shadow.

"Now put the knife down and hand me that phone, or I'll get Mr. Spade to do it for you!"

The knife is put down, and with the same hand and a grunt of discomfort he places the phone next to it.

Standing over him like an executioner there is only a small part of me that wants to kill him. I believe myself capable of the act but not in cold blood, not when there are alternatives.
"Good lad," I say patronisingly.
"Now this is what I'm going to do. I'm going to leave you here for a couple of hours and then because I'm a good guy I'm going to phone an ambulance for you. I suggest that you use the time to think up the least damaging reason why you have fallen down these stairs."
"I'm fucked up bad, I need to go to hospital now," he protests his face all sweaty and ashen.
"You can wait an hour or so ... look at it as penance for your crimes, or if you've got the balls for it you could drag yourself out."

The situation is a can of worms - all of it, top to bottom and there is no clear way out without getting tripped, stuck or caught. It is a proper bloody mess that can't be tidied up. I scoop the knife and phone up with the spade and trudge up the stairs, followed by the dog killer's blood lipped pleas,
"You will phone won't you? I'll keep my mouth shut I promise ... please."
I drop the phone on the way up and leave the knife cleaned at the top of the stairs – I'd give him options.

While I had deliberated taking a man's life Toni had found the car keys. We meet in the lounge and she jangles the keys for me to see with a big crooked grin on her face. I smile weakly, assailed by second thoughts. I am standing at the crossroads – the Rubicon in front. If I leave with Toni in the Ranger it will have been crossed. I inhale deeply through my nose inflating my lungs to their limit. I hold the breath a moment and then slowly exhale – sometimes it doesn't pay to think too much. Sometimes you are better off not thinking at all.

CHAPTER 15

The street is clear, and Toni leads the way to the Ranger carrying the metal detector and some other useful things she has scavenged. I limp behind and use the spade as an improvised walking stick, to lessen the weight on a now throbbing shin. She has the engine running by the time I get in. I chuck the spade and rucksack across the back seat and roll up the warm wet leg of my jeans. In the centre of my hairy shin there is a jagged hole about a quarter of an inch long. The whole shin is smeared with blood and the hairs are flattened and caked. A light trickle of blood works towards the boot. The outer side of the calf is gashed like an obscene grin and that too bleeds. Twenty-three years of managing mutants on the streets of South Wales and I had never been stabbed – and now on a holiday in Iceland of all places – the irony is not missed.

"Once we are out of here I'll take a look at that. I swiped some bandages and antiseptic from Jon's medicine cabinet. Nurse Toni will take care of you."

She winks and smiles suggestively, and I am left feeling what that smile couldn't do.

Street lights zip past as we head south out of Isafjordur. Around us the night sky is sharp, clean black and starry. Behind us in the distance, out at sea, I can make out the faint green shimmer of the Northern Lights. I had meant to see them and now they fade in the rear-view mirror. At a junction Toni ignores the dividing line and cuts right through. She guns the engine and we leave the light of the Fjord, ploughing through the darkness disappearing into the mountains.

"Is the cockroach dead?" she asks, her face dripping with disdain.

"About halfway there," I reply with an odd sense of shame at not finishing the job and risking her disapproval.

"Difficult to say what would be best. If I had hit him with the axe I don't think I would have been able to stop," she says reflectively.

"It's worrying to know that someone who is maybe my girlfriend is a potential axe murderer."

"It's on my dating profile enjoys candle lit dinners, long romantic walks and dismemberment."

I guffaw like a hyena, her humour cracked me up.

"And you are a fine one to talk walking around with that spade ... people in glass houses and all that."

"True, I can't argue with that, can't argue with it at all."

A dozen or so miles out of town we pull off the road onto a gravel track and kill the lights. I open the passenger door and hear the engine tinging with heat. I sit sideways and Toni comes around and kneels at my feet.

"Has your phone got a torch app?" she asks.

I switch it on and under the light she cleans and bandages my wounds like some kind of alternative angel, and a powerful swell of emotion flutters my heart.

"That should do it."

I look at her longingly,

"A kiss will really make it better."

She rises, grips the back of my neck and we lock in a passionate kiss. Then she breaks off leaving me wanting more. Radiating heat, she oozes,

"We got business to take care of ... we'll play later."

We get back onto the road and continue south west along a route called Vestfjaroarvegur. I shrink the map and scroll, speculating where we may be travelling to.

"Before you ask where we are going – it's Svalvogar. I heard Jon say it is a Fjord on the west coast and it is near a lighthouse there. In our haste to get out of town I don't even know I'm heading in the right direction," and she laughs carelessly like a cavalier.
"I'll find out."
I type it into the Google map and hit search. A blue line springs south from our location to a small town called Pingeyri. It then bends west onto a road called the 622 which runs along the coastline out onto a peninsula. It tells me that it is sixty-two kilometres and an hour and ten minutes away. I research it and Svalvogar isn't a place, it is a circular route between two fjords starting and ending at Pingeyri and is forty-nine kilometres long.

I look at the map again and the area resembles the gnarled, mutilated fingers of two splayed hands placed next to one another. Then I look again, and it doesn't, it really doesn't. I had in that moment just seen it that way. I take my glasses off and put the phone back in the coat pocket. It had been long day both awful and great.

At such times the Nadurra or one of its brethren calls, and more often than not I answer; and tonight, I reach into my bag for that beautiful bottle. My shin aches and I give myself the excuse that it is medicinal. I pop the top and take a deep slug straight from the source. I have an intimacy with whisky where it is no longer necessary for the intermediary of a glass. I kiss the bottle and it kisses back.

"You're fond of Scotch then?" she comments in a half humorous, half judgemental way that men and women in relationships reserve for one another.

"Whatever gives you that idea?"
I say, grinning and feigning innocence before kissing the lips of the bottle for another hit of the sweet, amber burn. In minutes I am in what I call the lift off zone where you feel the thrusters of the drug behind you, propelling you upwards out of tiredness, doubt and discomfort. I should try and cool my engines and stop here longer, but invariably I don't.

The white lines on the road are eaten up by our speed and soon we drop down onto the coastal road of a fjord. There is a small settlement with scattered lights over the water that I think is Pingeyri. The moon reflects off the dark, choppy water as we wind around the inlet towards the bridge that will take us across.

"I've got to come clean on something," I say.

"You married, got an STD ... are a Scientologist?" she bursts out with derisory laughter.

"Because I think I'd rather the first two."

"No, none of those I'm not a Firefighter ... I'm a Police Sergeant," and I wait for a reaction.

Her face doesn't drop like it could have and there isn't a concealing silence to pack true feelings away.

"My uncle Warren was a cop and I've got a cousin Liz who is one too; why didn't you tell me from the get-go?"

"Because I wanted to forget I am one ... it weighs on me sometimes and ... I just want to drop the load and be something else. When we first spoke, I had no idea it would turn into this."

"No one could have predicted this. I hit on you for wrong reasons ... but I guess it just goes to show that sometimes good can come out of bad," and she pouts and ripples her mouth the same as a cheeky wink of an eye.

"Everything else I told you Toni is the truth," I say slowly wanting the words to have gravity, to fall out of the air with their weight.

"Naw it's cool, it explains a lot actually, about why you stepped in and protected me ... like a guard dog."

I gaze out of the window at the dense black mountains silhouetted against a less black sky and remark to myself as much as to Toni.

"More like an old dog clinging onto the hunt, loyal to a master that no longer wants him."

"You've lost me a bit with that metaphor Will."

"I ran into some grief in work with another asshat that likes to beat on women, and the cop that is investigating the complaint is determined to do my legs because it will make him look ethical. The logical side of me thinks I'll get through it, yet I'm nagged by an irrational dread that I won't."

"That sounds like anxiety Will. I got hit with a bullshit disciplinary when I was a nurse, and my reaction was to say fuck them and their job; and there was no anxiety because I didn't care. I chose not to play their game. Be your own man Will, determine your own fate, it's liberating."

I heard words that I needed to hear and an attitude that I needed to have. Our eyes meet and another hook pierces my skin.

The bridge is a narrow strip of road laid low over the water and has piled rocks for sides. We shoot across, the night ours, the landscape dead but for us. The half-cut moon illuminates like a weak spotlight, and the beams of the Ranger push back at the near pitch-black darkness of a land that has yet to be tamed. Through the night we storm towards Pingeyri, foot down, tearing at the bends, Toni locked in a duel with the road.

I have to flick the Fitbit twice to get the time: 7:43, but what does that mean out here doing this? It is midway through an afternoon shift, the time I usually woke up from a nap before a night shift, it was around the time Beth and I had sat down for supper. We are off the clock and now it is just a number on a screen.

The speedometer is nudging seventy miles per hour and the Ranger rolls on its sloppy suspension like a water bed on wheels. Houses and street lights appear, and Toni drops the speed. A quarter of a mile in, the road dips to the right, and I can see two red flags busily flapping in the wind in front of a forecourt.

"Toni there is a petrol station on the right."

"Got it."

The Ranger bisects the junction and pushes out onto the gravel, and the nearside tyres spit out chippings like machine gun fire. We drive onto the forecourt and I fill up, while Toni goes into the red framed shop to pay for the fuel and get supplies. On the other side of the road there is a small harbour and I watch the fishing boats gently bob and rock at the hand of a strong wind.

My buzz is easing, and I slip back in the Ranger to top up like the sly drinker I am. She gets back in and hands me a Red Bull which I take eagerly. It goes well with whisky and on many a work's night out I've blasted both.

"Is there a plan?" I ask.

"Of course not," she replies as if it were a dull question, and she tips her head back for the Red Bull.

"Thought as much they always go wrong anyway ... we'll wing it ... fly by the seat of our pants."

We hitch on to the 622 and at first it is little different from the Vestfjaroarvegur road. Then it starts to break up and get primitive like the farm tracks of home, except this road is carved out of the side of a mountain and drops into the sea.

"We'll stop here," she says with a note of exasperation,

"There's no point in going over a cliff is there."

"Drive to arrive ... that's something my first Sergeant said to me once and it stuck. There was a code red put out and everyone jumped in cars and vans and tore off to help the officer in trouble. Another police car overtook us like a lunatic and the Sarge said to me, Will, drive to arrive because you're no good to them wrapped around a lamp post."

"Yeah ... and the brooch is no use in the dark any ways. Let's get some shut eye, there'll be lots of shit to get through tomorrow."

"You don't say. If the last two days are anything to go by it will be a shit fest. You could have a side-line ... Toni's Alternative Tours: Fight Your Way Around Iceland."

I snigger at my own sarcasm and she joins in like a good sport.

"You just like the tour guide."

"Maybe, or perhaps I miss punching scumbags in the head."

I dropped the seat back, crossed my arms and nestled into my hood. I am enervated yet wired and far from sleep. 8:22, I have known her just shy of two days, and I am worried that I more than like her. What little judgement I have left is eroding, crumbling like a castle made of sand. I see it. I see it like a slow-motion car crash where there is a part of you that seeks the impact, seeks the carnage.

I segue onto Adam and where I left him busted up in the basement. I said I'd phone an ambulance for him and I should because it is the right thing to do. I fish out my phone and dial in the number - even vermin didn't deserve to suffer. My thumb hovers over the call icon but I don't press. In this situation right and smart aren't the same. My number could be traced even if I withheld it. This is a gamble and I'm not sure where to place my chips. If Adam is saved he may say nothing, and the case would be closed. If cops find him dead there will be a full-blown investigation and I'll get drawn into it because of the previous police report. If Adam manages to crawl free or Marcus went back to get him then it could work out. I put my phone away, in this situation doing the right thing is a bad bet.

"Fancy a cwtch in the back," I suggest.
"What's a cwtch dare I ask?" she replies.
"It's Welsh for a cuddle. It's going to get cold and we should conserve heat. I'd say this to you if you were a bit of a moose or a guy ... it's practical."
"You are such a sweet talker Will; you can tell you don't date."
I take the seat back up, put what is on the back seat into the boot and slide in. Toni joins me and we snuggle into one another.
"Where's that scotch?" she purrs her head resting on my heart.
I draw the bottle out and lament the missing half – it had been a hard trip full of extenuating circumstances and no doubt there would be more to come. We cwtch and sup whisky until eventually sleep overtakes us.

I sleep fitfully and it is a little after four when a dead leg wakes me. The pins and needles momentarily worsened by the blood flowing back into the leg. Toni's back is curled into my chest and she is sound asleep. I try to get back off to sleep but with the cold cramped conditions it doesn't come easy. I think about Beth and it is like flicking through a book of many chapters. I jump to significant points in time, and others inconsequential yet somehow remembered, so perhaps they have meaning after all. I jump to the beginning and stop at how we met.

It was a Saturday on a bank holiday weekend in late August 1990. I was out at the Sker with my best mate Jason, dressed up in tan chinos and white Pringle polo shirt worn tucked in. The evening was young and beautiful as we sat on the benches in front of the pub, taking in beer and the waning rays of sunshine. Jason's girlfriend Amanda came over with her friend Beth. Beth was a red-haired stunner with bee stung lips and the hands of a screen goddess – she was way, way out of my league and like a goddess I admired her from afar.

They sat down and as was my way I teased and took the piss, never for a moment thinking I was any more than the annoying friend. The night cracked on and we went our separate ways.

Later in a bar called The Accolade we all met up again. I had sunk close to ten pints and should have been more smashed than I was, but on some nights you just can't be put down. There was music I can't recall what and people were dancing, just dancing where they were. It was hot and crowded, and people were singing and swaying, now reduced by alcohol to who they were. Without a word she grabbed my hands, and stupidly we swung around like children. The tiled floor was greasy with spilt beer and inevitably we went over. She landed on top of me and tipped her glass of Pernod and black over my shirt. She was apologetic, though I couldn't have given a damn - she could have stained every shirt in my wardrobe, and I wouldn't have had a care - a door had opened that I thought was locked to me.

It was time to move onto Wall Street a nightclub of the time, and as we left she led me by the hand out into the car park. I remember thinking whatever is happening I'd better make the most of it, because it will probably never happen again. I stopped and pulled her towards me. I placed my hands around her tiny waist my fingers but inches from touching each other. Then I kissed those soft, plump lips and for the rest of the night I couldn't let her go. I later learned what she liked about me – she liked that I was a charmless man. That I hadn't pawed and fed her oily lines like many others had. I wouldn't have known how.

CHAPTER 16

I had managed to drift back off and grab pieces of sleep, but I was far from refreshed. Light from behind the mountains had lifted the lid of darkness and brought in the dawn. I got out of the car and stretched, my mouth feeling that something had crawled inside it and died. It is sharply cold, and I am in dire need of a very hot mug of coffee, which it doesn't look like I'm going to get out here. I decide to make do with a Red Bull, waking Toni as I rummage in the bag. I hand her one also and joke,
"Here get some wings."
She yawns and drags the sleep from her eyes.
"After that night's sleep I need rocket fuel," her voice husky and scratched by the night's whisky.
"Adrenaline will do it. I think I've enough left in the tank to carry me one more day before I'm frazzled."
I open the boot and sit on the sill to change underwear. I then take my toothbrush and paste out of my rucksack and using the spade as a stick carefully make my way down the bank to the Fjord. The wind has calmed and the water laps softly over the stony dirt. I notice further along the shoreline a solitary tree, bent and blanched white dead with a crow perching on one of the cracked branches. The crow caws, opening and closing its knife-like beak and I wonder how many sheep's eyes had been pecked out with it – then I wonder if a crow would have mine, would get to dine on my face on the side of some windswept mountain.
I wash and clean and the freezing water jolts me alert and ex-

cites the cold to nip at my face. I find a sheep track and struggle back to the Ranger, and Toni passes me on the way. Back at the Ranger I eat a peanut butter and chocolate bar thinking that she seemed fond of these. Toni returns and we get going.

The road is roughly hewn and is really no more than a thick mountain bike track. It requires full attention and is in parts like walking a tightrope. I drive slowly and delicately across the waist of the mountain, showing due respect, trying not to anger it lest it flip us off. We are quiet and tense, our eyes fixed just beyond the bonnet glued to the minutiae of the road. The Ranger rocks over the bumps and the water dark in the shadow of the mountain waits. A buckle in the road lifts the inside wheel and turns it out, and the Ranger lurches towards the edge. I slam on the brakes and we stop facing the horizon.

"Whoa!" I expel.

"Been driving long," she ribbed.

I make a face like it is funny but barely so. I then reverse and re-align the Ranger and we roll on. Hugging the mountainside and keeping a safe margin from the edge, moving slow and steady through the ruts and ridges.

The cabin feels like a pressure cooker until we trundle off the mountain and the road pulls away from the lip of the cliff.

"Why couldn't this treasure be buried a few yards off the Ring Road hey?"

She comes back at me in the tone of an old school Ma'am,

"Because it wouldn't be as much fun Will. Now don't be a grumpy old man."

"I'd like to become a grumpy old man."

Though this is only half true; I'm kind of indifferent to making old bones.

We pass a pimped, green Volkswagen T5 camper van at the side of the road. Two men wearing bright anoraks, cargo shorts and tights underneath are at the back end of it prepping fat wheeled mountain bikes.

"Looks like we aren't the only fools out here," she says absently as if the greater part of her mind is absorbed in untangling a dense knot.

There are wilder more remote places in the world, but here on a sparsely populated jut of rock on the very western edge of Europe, facing an expanse of ocean and the emptiness Greenland beyond, it felt that foul deeds could be done, and how easy it would be for no one to get to know of them.

I'd been mulling a question in my head that I am uncertain I want the answer to. I suppose I do want to ask it, only I don't want a real ugly reply.

"I know money is certainly the answer; it is the motivation for most of the things people do, but you have a business that you love, why do you want to risk everything on what is likely a wild goose chase?"

"I could ask the same of you, and from where I'm sitting you've got more to lose than me."

"Yes, you could but I asked first," I said childishly invoking the law of the playground.

"Finding it would make my father proud of me. I'd complete a journey that he started ..."

Toni tails off, seemingly unconvinced by her own story and then pulls the plug on it altogether. There is an uncomfortable pause which I don't fill. I give her time to get a grip on what she is about to say. Toni sucks her top lip and says,

"I need the money. I incurred debts setting up the shop and it is proving hard keeping my head above water. North Tonawanda has three ink shops and there are plenty of others nearby in Cheektowaga, Niagara Falls, Lockport and Buffalo. I got the loan on the new equipment, rent for the shop, rent for my apartment and the beat-up old car I drive keeps needing repairs. To add to this my father is sick and the medical insurance doesn't cover all the bills. I make money but I don't make enough."

"What about Marcus?" I ask.

"Marcus Rocher, he's got his own financial problems. A big chunk of his cash goes up his nose and he loses more at the track and at the poker table. When I told him, he wasn't nearly as sceptical as you."

"A drowning man will clutch at straws that's why, buy into any pipe dream. What about Jon, what is he in it for ... glory or coin?"

"Jon's broke. He hasn't said as much but he says his pension from the Fisheries Department doesn't stretch far, and he complains about the upkeep costs on his boat. How about you, how are you fixed for money?"

"I'm good at the minute though I could have some worries down the line."

I then realize that I hadn't given much thought to the financial aspect of losing my job. We had lived within our means and didn't owe anything to anybody, however that was with a Sergeant's wage. If they sent me down the road I wouldn't get close to that - I'd be earning peanuts stacking shelves somewhere. Maybe I ought to take a fair cut and then it wouldn't matter what I did.

After a jarring ride we reach the point of the peninsula and the track bears left across its rocky crown. Gulls sail high on the winds above and swoop like dive bombers into the sea. An undulating dark iron sea ripping white across the surface and pounding furiously into the shore. I see the lighthouse and a spike of adrenaline comes with it. Expectantly I survey the uneven, craggy terrain and disappointingly that is all there is.

The lighthouse is different from the tall white towers dotting the coast of the British Isles. With a red housing on top and a yellow support block underneath it appears dumpy by comparison. I notice an integral metal rung ladder running up the side to a platform where the housing is set. I stop the Ranger next to it.

"This is a good vantage point," I say. "If they are nearby we should be able to spot them."

"And them us," she retorts.

"No risk no reward," I encourage, smiling at my memories of this in action.

The wind ruffles our clothing trying to cause mischief as we climb up the bare metal rungs to the platform. On top I smell the salt in the unspoiled air and listen to the cries of the gliding gulls.

Toni adjusts the binoculars to her eyes and scopes the landscape.

"Any sign?" I ask.

"Nope, just a lot of shit spattered rocks."

There isn't the time or mood to appreciate the view and we climb back down to the Ranger.

Back in the cab I break open another Red Bull and say to Toni, "Are you sure of the location?"

"Yes. I heard Jon talking about Svalvogar and the lighthouse and it is near there, so it must be further on. They can't have found and dug it up yet."

Toni squints her eyes a little, her brow furrowing in question of her recollection. I had often doubted that most fallible of our faculties myself. There were events I had forgotten and memories of things I'm pretty sure I'd imagined. Playfully I offer,

"Do you think the gambler pressed his luck and drove through the night?"

"He might have, or he could have gone back for Adam and be behind us."

"That didn't work out so well last time," I reply.

It felt like a game of cat and mouse, where the cat and mouse switched around – one day Tom the other day Jerry, and sooner or later whoever is Jerry is going to get fucked for good.

"Let's go on," she says.

"Aye, aye Captain," and we roll on.

CHAPTER 17

Jacked on caffeine and nervous energy twenty mile per hour is just too slow when you need to cut loose, and I'm piling up on myself like a derailed train. I grip the steering wheel and exert forces on it, venting my frustration when we hit another hairy section of the route and the speedometer drops down to five. I blow air through my nose like a bull, and keep my hands throttling the wheel, instead of beating and breaking something.

We reach a stretch of clear track and pick up speed and I start to loosen up a little. Then the road tilts downward in a long gradual descent along the margin of the Fjord. The sun having poked out from the white puffy clouds shimmers on the wrinkled water, and you could almost forget what you are here for. The thick tread tyres chew up the dry dirt into a dust cloud and we cut through a nascent, shallow stream that has yet to properly scar the mountain. The road runs to a point and ahead I see an odd rock formation. The mountain slopes and stops abruptly, there is a gap, sizeable as a mythic gateway and then a huge nub of rock like a bolt stiff nipple the other side - and what is beyond is unknown.

I push down on the accelerator and steer towards it, racing the sheer faced mountain wall that looms over us threatening to crash like a Hawaiian wave. I take my foot off the gas and ease through the passage and still almost smash into it. The tyres crunch the rocky dust and the Ranger comes to a halt less than twenty yards away.

It is stationary and askew as if it had come to a stop in a rush. For a split second I don't fully process what I see. A vacant gunmetal Mitsubishi Warrior the underbelly and flanks coated with dust and dirt, the rear right door dinked and scuffed of paint. I double check that my eyes haven't deceived me and that it is empty. Meanwhile, Toni flings opens the door and leaps out like she is parachuting from a plane. She strides towards the Warrior and elegantly skips into a twirl like some love-struck teenager, her head canted to the cliff top, her ice blue eyes taking everything in.

I get out and pull the spade off the back seat and stand guard. I watch Toni's right hand dip into a jacket pocket and take something out. I see both hands together at work and hear a faint snap. She places a spread hand against the rear door and stabs the tyre rapidly in three places. She leaves the tyre hissing from puncture wounds and moving onto the front tyre, swiftly injects it with steel. Amid a cacophony of sibilating air, she whips around the other side and bleeds out the other two. I am wrongfully impressed and keep lookout less than I ought.

She struts back wearing a lopsided grin, the lock knife in hand; its black blade compact and business like.

"That's them fucking stranded," she declares proudly.

"Done like a boss," I compliment.

"Am I the boss then?"

"I suppose you are, I'm dancing to your tune aren't I?"

"And do you like the tune?" she asks vampishly.

I stick my tongue into my bottom lip and shake my head.

"Stop fishing for compliments we've got a bad guy to find."

"They've likely climbed over the hill to find the exact location," and she waves yonder across the ridgeline.

I wander over to the Warrior, take off a glove and put the palm of my hand on the bonnet. It is lukewarm and I figure that the engine underneath has been idle for twenty to thirty minutes. I walk back to Toni and say,

"It would be a good idea if we hide the Ranger or they could do the same to us."

I swing back into the cab, make a three-point turn and exit the ravine. I take the Ranger three hundred or so yards up the track and park it in a nook where it widens. Toni pushes the twined axe handle into her rucksack leaving the small, dark age head partially exposed underneath the flap. The metal of which is weathered grey and chipped - chipped perhaps over a millennium ago splitting open the skull of an enemy.

We hike back with Toni carrying the metal detector and I with the spade in support. I am cautious going through the ravine and my eyes search the top in anticipation of being clobbered by a hurled rock. Toni sees a thin sheep track staggered on the hill and we make for it. The shin aches and bitches more today and I wince with nearly every steep step. Pain sweat appears on my brow and breaks out on my back in a flush, and I am sure by this stage I stink. I plod on, harassed by doubts I'm not up to the fight ahead.

Near the top I lower into a crouch and then go on to my knees and my shin hurts less. At the peak I lay on my front and prop myself up with an elbow. I use the binoculars and take time scoping the ground. The top doesn't level for far before there is a long escarpment to a low interceding hill with a rise beyond it. I sweep the binoculars the full field of view and don't see anything. I am about to get up when I see figures emerging from above the low hill climbing the rise to its twin peaks. The peaks are almost identical and look like two waves at their zenith rolling inland. I'm thinking that it is a unique feature when Toni whispers excitedly,

"That is it, the mountain with the curling peaks ... that is it!"

CHAPTER 18

At times twelve magnification I can see them clearly. There is Marcus in his svelte, ribbed jacket with a spade slung across his shoulder, a stooped, shaggy haired old man in a brown duffle coat, and the mysterious woman with a Mediterranean complexion, outfitted in grey carrying a detector. I watch Marcus hand the old man an object. I get a better perspective seeing the old man marvel at the brooch as he inspects it through a range of angles. He holds it up framing it against the mountain, then steps back, and moves sideways like he is trying to take the perfect camera shot. I then see old man Einarsson shake his grey white mane and point ahead. They continue, and I am worried to see Marcus tackling the hill with the grace of a gazelle. The woman is lithe too and Einarsson, though slower is still spry.

Toni wriggles in beside me.

"What can you see?"

"Marcus has given Jon the brooch and he has been trying to line it up. I think they are making their way over to the other side of the summit."

"I've been examining the terrain Will and there is a flatter, easier route to the left."

I look myself and could see that we are on the rim of a wonky bowl. To our left the rim rose sharply and then swept gently downward for the most part, curving into the shoulder of the twin peak mountain opposite. They had dropped into the bowl to frame the brooch, but the quicker route is around the rim.

"I like it Toni, we can flank them and if we pick our spot well, maybe we get the drop on them," and as I said it I knew it to be a long shot on open, barren ground.

We wait for them to disappear over the other side. Toni withdraws the axe and starts slaying the air with practice chops and slashes. Her face is steeled and prepared for mayhem, her strong arms and core handling the axe with ease. Watching her it is evident that a light, utilitarian axe is simply better at swiftly hacking a resisting human being to pieces, than the ponderous, oversized battle axes beloved of fantasy – and I ruminate that appearances can be deceptive, and like many things in life less is often more.

"Got an axe to grind?" I quip not able to resist the awful pun, and as I've come to expect she is lightning quick on the comeback.

"No, I'm the forgiving sort I'm going to bury the hatchet," she replies with not so innocent sincerity.

"Where though that's what concerns me," I say dryly.

"I'm a perfect nightmare, an ex with an axe."

And I had to agree this was going to go sideways no two ways about it.

We set off armed with a piece of Viking history and a garden tool, and in my mind I hear the dice clinking in the shot glass. I call on the last reserves of adrenaline and we cover the ground, watched over by a low autumn sun squinting through gaps in thin monochrome cloud. When we get close I slip off my coat and gloves to be unencumbered as possible and drop to my haunches. Toni copies me stripping light and before I can signal for her to drop down she does. I cradle the spade like it were my rifle and commando crawl over the cold, dewy grass to the ridgeline of the mountain's shoulder.

I peek over, and the descent on the other side is a kind sweep over scrubby grass, that is balding with dirt and pimpled with small gnarled rock. The woman now has the brooch held in front of her like it is a camera phone and Marcus is nowhere to be seen. Jon stands behind her with his hands stuffed into coat pockets dejectedly staring downward into the ground. If Adam was sent to dispose of Toni then would what they had planned for Jon be any different? And did he suspect as they zeroed in on the prize that his minutes were now numbered, like sand grains seeping through a flipped hourglass? Perhaps he contemplates the hole dug to get the gold, will serve another purpose and become an anonymous grave.

I divert my attention from Jon and the woman and search the slope for Marcus. I can't see him, and a prick of panic makes me think he is on to us and could be outflanking us now. I spin around and startle Toni and my alarm is infectious. Our eyes rake the terrain like a pair of cross-eyed antennae until we are satisfied that we are safe for the moment, however fleeting that moment maybe. I get back into position and when Marcus appears at the woman's side, I realize that he had merely been eclipsed by her.

The woman nods her head, and Marcus with the detector and the spade in each hand hikes diagonally up the hill in our direction. I press the left side of my face into the earth and hear my heart thump inside my ear, and the fast, thumping beats become a tense metronome. Is he going to climb over the shoulder and stumble over us I fret? I think, and remember the cross is south east of the peaks. I give it a long minute and edge my eye over to see Marcus walking backwards up the hill. He stops and takes several pronounced sidesteps to his left. He then paces a dozen steps forward and two further sidesteps left.

"There, stop there!" the woman hollers.

Marcus holds the spot and discards the spade. With his back to me he fiddles with the detector and I think about making my move. I cast a practised eye over the distance and estimate the range to the target to be between sixty and seventy yards. There is absolutely no cover for a stalk, and I envisage the odds of reaching him with a mad charge down the hill before he would notice. Slim chance of that - about the same as a smack head making his job seekers allowance last two weeks. Marcus would notice, but would he have enough time to effectively react to a shock assault?

Marcus takes a packet out of his pocket and hinges the lid open. He puts his lips to the top and pulls out a cigarette. The packet goes back and out comes a zip lighter which flames with a sharp flick of the wrist. The cigarette is lit, and a puff of smoke rises, and with the cigarette perched from his lips he swings the detector in arcs over the ground in ever increasing circles. I continue to watch transfixed if he will find the prize.

"What's happening?" whispers Toni.

"They've found the spot and Marcus is using the detector to locate it. Get ready to go!"

From a one eyed slant I see Marcus suddenly stop mid swing and hover the detector in small circles. He shouts excitedly down the hill,

"I found something!"

He places the detector down and I realize he's going back for the spade and that the ideal moment is passing. With my palms pressed into the earth I explode to my feet and sprint down the mountain. The sky shakes, my shin bursts pain and my breath comes hard and bloody in the cold morning air. I grimace hurt, I grimace grief, I grimace war, I grimace the point of my existence where it could end - I hurtle down the hill right on the edge of falling.

At thirty yards I see Marcus lean for the spade, stubby cigarette in mouth, his tattooed hand grasping for the handle. Four to five seconds and I will be on him with the decisive blow. At twenty-five I suddenly see the rock, a bulbous rock the size of a big beach ball lodged in the ground, just three yards in front. I adjust my step and leap for it with my good leg. I plant my foot on the top and push off. I hit the ground and a spasm of pain shoots upwards through my bad leg. I stumble wonky legged and bent over fighting to stay on my feet. I steady and raise my head somewhere between twenty and fifteen yards. I see Marcus open mouthed and aghast, the almost spent cigarette dropping from his lips. I hear a war scream from behind, and Marcus is on his heels back peddling, tripping over, rolling off his back and on to his feet, turning tail and running.

For a half-second I almost had him as he scrambled up to his feet, though in the next half-second he was able to stretch away; my short, injured legs no match for his long gait.

Further down Jon has made a break for it, he heads to us, the grey woman in close pursuit. She grabs a hold of the hood of the duffle coat and she spins him with velocity to the ground. With powerful strides Toni overtakes me, the head of the axe bobbing with derangement in her hand; and I have to dig deep to keep up. Jon gets to his feet and the woman pounces on his back dragging him to the ground like a savannah lion. Marcus makes a beeline for them, the distance opening up between us. Jon struggles to his knees, the woman's arms hooked around his hips, his bearded face a picture of anguish. Marcus closes in, deftly turning one hundred and eighty degrees in front of Jon and executing a snappy back hand hammer fist to the temple poleaxes the old man. Marcus steps back over Jon and raises the spade over his spread-eagled body, the blade poised as a guillotine above his throat.

The woman her hand fumbling in her trouser pocket retreats behind Marcus. Toni quick foots to a stop, her eyes darting between the kidnappers. I draw alongside her, feeling I want to nail him bad for sparking out a defenceless old man.

"That's it hold yer horses," says Marcus smugly, his grin failing as he tries to bring his breathing under control.

"Not a move or Jon boy here loses part of his head. Toni, you know I'll do it, and you! whoever the fuck you are? you know, you know what I'm about."

I do, it is no bluff. He would drive the spade through the old guy's head like it was a breakfast egg. The same as he would trample over a child to get out of a burning building – just sacks of meat getting in his way. Marcus is Nicky Larkin two point zero, developed, upgraded next tier. My policing experience has given me a Layman's appreciation of personality types, and Marcus is a psychopath, or at least a full-blown sociopath on his way to a promotion.

There is a click and the woman steps forward alongside Marcus holding a knife, the sharp end a serrated four inches. We are now standing in a rough square a little less than a dozen yards apart. Eleven yards separating negotiation and the world of words from bloodletting and primal law.

"That's my father's brooch, he found it, you've got no right to it Marcus."

"Might is right bitch, and the brooch don't give a shit who's holding it."

He smirks and dismissively shakes his head chiding her.

"That's lame Toni you're going to have to do better than that girl."

Wounded by his barbed words she fires back,

"Is she your new punch bag?"

The woman bristling with anger rocks her head side to side and spits,

"No, you skanky puta I'm his fiancée."

She is the youngest of us all being I guess in her late twenties. She stands around five feet five and is like a stick with it. Her angular looks are attractive, but devoid of softness and marred by a hunger for something she never had. The flinty stare she is giving Toni tells she has something to prove.

Marcus cocks his head over in my direction and says with a snigger,

"If you haven't worked it out dumbo, she's a crazy chick, real loop the loop. You'll have fun, you'll just have to learn to sleep with one eye open is all."

Bridled, Toni takes a half-step forward the axe straining in her hand. The situation is turning into a four way domestic ding dong with the old man hostage to the overspill. It is time for me to remember who I am.

"Okay Marcus let's take this down a notch or two. I don't want

Jon to get hurt so we'll back off."

"No Will!" dissents Toni.

"Yes, Toni we have to."

"Listen to your boy Toni, he's talking sense. Back up and drop your weapons and the old man gets to mumble on about shit another day."

His smoker's voice is full of inflection and malice, but the impenetrable pools of black that are his eyes are shark dead.

"Fuck you!"

"Ah that's the Toni I know."

"Move on him Conchita and I'll fucking slice your eyes out."

The woman sounded New York streets, spiky, vivacious, Latino. Her kite shaped face sets into an ugly scowl and the knife in her hand seems restless for action.

"Nice Marta. See Toni that's what loyalty looks like."

I bring the conversation back on track.

"No, we keep hold of the weapons only a naive fool with a death wish would give them up."

"I want the weapons. I don't want any more nasty surprises," he insists.

Deadpan I counter,

"Look Marcus, I know you'll kill Jon if you need to, and I don't want you to kill him, but you're overplaying your hand if you think I give that much of a fuck."

"Well, what we have here then is a good old, fashioned Mexican standoff," replies Marcus almost jovial.

"Yes, we do, but the fact is you are outgunned. That axe beats her piddly knife all day long. All I must do is keep you occupied for twenty seconds then it is two on one. And then you'll have an ex-girlfriend full of piss and vinegar at your back with an axe."

He tried to poker face it, but I saw it hit home. I'd found a chink in the bravado. Though cocksure and arrogant he isn't stupid. The stupid didn't recognize a tight spot when they were in one, however he did.

"But I handled you so easily last time that I was embarrassed for you, and there is no little fall to save you here. You are a skill less brawler, whereas I have trained at the birthplace of Karate in Okinawa. You are simply out of your depth, and with the spade it will be one strike," he says with a narcissist's certainty.

He is trying to get under my skin with the bravado, to score a psychological victory with his swagger so the fight goes the same way. It doesn't work I know what I got to do, just hang in there and wait for Toni to come through.

The situation is charged, and the air practically crackles as though a dynamo is being furiously cranked into the red. My eyes flit from one powder keg to another trying to figure who will be the one to strike the match.

"We could split the treasure five ways," offers Toni out of left field.

"Really!" replies Marcus elongating the word as if he is having trouble digesting what Toni had just said.

"Yeah, walking away with a fifth is a better option than us butchering one another and leaving the treasure with the mountain."

"Six ways. It would need to be six ways for Adam to get a share too."

Amid the tension there is a note of relief. He hadn't died, or maybe he had, and Marcus is cutting himself a bigger slice of the pie – who knows, at this rate I could guess and double guess in a matter of a second or two.

"He's still alive then?" I look to confirm.

"Yes, no thanks to you."

And through the corner of his left eye I am needled with a baleful stare.

"All right we'll split it fifty-fifty, a half for each side," Toni agrees with a palpable reluctance.

"Also no more talking to the cops. We've both taken hits and everyone's hands are dirty. Adam had a hit and run traffic accident, Jon lost his keys and had to break into his own house, and you Toni wanted to come along for the ride. Getting the cops involved hurts everyone and they'll end up finding out what we're after," proposes Marcus and what he said made sense – lines had been crossed on both sides.

There is complicit silence, and no one moves. This plan requires trust and it is in short supply and I am reminded of the fable *The Scorpion and the Frog*. In our version they are the scorpion and we are the frog and they will sting us crossing the river, even if in doing so it would drown us all. I glance at Toni, her jaw tight, her intense blue eyes boring holes; then it occurs to me that maybe it is only me that is the frog.

Still no one moves. My mind whirs frantically thinking of how to simultaneously save Jon and backtrack out of a deal that gets our heads bashed in the first moment our guards are lowered. The ominous silence continues; though the feverish calculations and machinations, being made behind these sets of shifty eyes could almost be heard. I feel compelled to speak yet I don't know what to say.

"You direct and we'll dig," suggests Toni.

"Yeah we should keep ap .. art," I say wincing as a casual adjustment in stance throbs suffering through my lower leg.

Marcus smiles a closed lipped smile that barely turns up at the edges.

"My boy hurt you with the knife didn't he? Knife like that would cut to the bone. Give the man some respect though, you got some dog in you to still be here."

"You better believe it," and I could feel emotion welling up from the gut.

Then in an absolute moment of clarity I realize what it is all about, what it has ever been about - the fight: the ring, the streets, the mountain - the guns had to blaze win, lose or draw.

"Go up the hill then already," orders Marta, hand on hip in a strop and her eyes burning with impatience.

Jon comes around with a startled expression and I see him roll from underneath the blade before Marcus does. He rolls towards us like a log and the spade is driven into the earth behind him. I move, rushing forward ignoring pain as Marcus hefts and plunges the spade at Jon. It slices downward scagging the duffel coat as he spins, pegging a part of it into the ground. Jon suddenly stops, cries out and crosses his arms in front of his face.

"Marcus!" shouts Marta.

Marcus looks up in time to see me bull towards him with the spade at the point of the charge. The split second before impact with all the force I can muster I thrust the spade at his chest. With cat like reflexes Marcus pivots at the hips swerving his upper body to the right, while bringing up the shaft of the spade to parry. The spades clatter loudly as the shaft catches the blade diverting it upwards. I follow through crashing into him, going underneath the shaft and smashing him in the mouth with the handle of the spade. His head jolts back and to the right, and he is lifted off his feet and sent rudely to the ground. He falls on his side and rolls with the momentum onto his knees, his back to me and with the spade tenuously held and outstretched in front of him. Securing a foot in the earth he starts to rise, as I move in to kill the space and finish.

Pushing off the foot Marcus rotates violently to his right, and I sense it just in time as I enter the firing line of a do or die back swing. The spade arcs towards my head and if I hesitate or falter I'm dead. I hurl myself forward to beat the blade and get ahead of it. I do and the wood above his hand hits harmlessly into my upper arm. With the spade as a crossbar I ram it into the right side of his ribcage sending him flying like a crash test dummy. He nosedives into the wet grass, his legs folding over his back like a Scorpion's tail. I hear screams behind me, and I shut them out.

I close, and as he is gathering his limbs to spring back up I spear the ankle of the trailing leg. There is a head turning crunch accompanied by an unrestrained yawp that carries over the hills. Marcus bends to the pain, clasping his ankle he rocks on his back, glaring with astonished eyes and clenched teeth. He grabs for the spade and I raise mine as though I'm going to split a log. I propel the executioner's axe and I see death shroud his face - a capture of when the light is about to be snuffed out. He recoils in horror, palms upward in submission and I halt the blade two feet above his head.

"Nah this won't do. I want to fight you mano-o-mano, your skills against mine. Get up!"
I step back to give us both room. He warily sits up, coughs and says shakily,
"You're as crazy as she is."
"What are you doing Will?" and I hear Toni's voice coming from somewhere behind me.
"Have you ever gotten something you didn't deserve? It comes cheaply and has a hollow ring. I beat you but I hit you below the belt to do it. Now I'm going to beat you fairly. We're going to stand facing each other with our fucked up legs and fight until one of us goes down and doesn't get back up."
In the pit of my stomach emotions writhed then soared liked fireworks.
"No Will that's fucking insane, smash the other leg and cripple the fucker, and be done with it."
"Where's Marta?" asks Marcus.
"I slashed her arm, and she ran like a frightened little bitch," boasts a pissed and triumphant Toni.
He looks up at her and I think I detect a hint of concern, then again it could be for himself. He pushes more,
"Badly?"
"Nuh, it's not hanging off or anything; should be a nasty gash though and leave a pretty scar," she answers him with relish.
Marcus's face sours with an expression of contempt.
"I bet she hasn't told you about the time she stabbed me in the ass with a steak knife for turning up late."
He hacks up another cough and the dead, black eyes twinkle with devilment.
"Fucking five hours I waited for you, let's not get into war stories

I got more than you, you piece of shit."
"Managed to kill the time though didn't you by snorting a few lines and getting well into a second bottle of wine, all on top of the happy pills you are always popping. Time I got round she was a fucking train wreck. I almost pity you fella, you don't know what you've got yourself into."

Over the years I'd been to hundreds of domestic arguments and I am a part of one now. A relationship could end yet enmity could keep it going like pouring petrol on a flagging fire. It is recent and still raw between these two with a gang of grudges lining up on each side to settle score. They were volatile together and probably loved hard, now in love's aftermath they are hating with the same passion.

Only now do I notice that Jon has got up and is standing slightly behind me. His long fingers touch his temple and he examines it for blood. He doesn't say anything, though I suspect he has a lot of things to say and is letting this storm pass before saying them.

"Will, is that your name? What's your story fella? why have you got yourself mixed up in this shit? You're from England right? ... you two meet online, have one of those sad long, distance relationships?"

He had calmed his fear and was now talking in an easy relaxed manner as if he hadn't a care in the world.

"No, met the old fashion way in a bar three days ago."

"Huh, Huh, damn that's mighty quick work Toni I'm impressed, how you can get some random guy to go through so much shit. So, I ask again are you in it for the pussy or the cash?"

"Neither."

Puzzlement temporarily replaces contempt and I want him to know what I'm about.

"I'm in it for the action. Speaking of which are we going to fight, or do I punish you where you sit?

"Punish me for what? she owes me money, she wouldn't be here if I hadn't bankrolled this trip. I'm not afraid to fight you, but isn't it stupid that men are always fucking each other up because of women?"

"Beat his ass Will," urges Toni snatching the spade up.

"Huh see, and with her on the side-lines even if I win I lose," he says disgruntled and shaking his head.

"My heart bleeds for you. Enough talk, let's go."

"You've got a white knight complex bud and it's going to get you killed."

With some discomfort Marcus gets to his feet and tests his right ankle with small movements. He removes his jacket and rolls up the sleeves of a black Yojimbo sweater with the words "Come Get Some" woven on the chest. I throw the spade behind me, get into a crouched boxing stance and clench my fists. Marcus points to a piece of relatively flat stone less ground of piebald green and brown. I nod and we carry ourselves over to our arena, a facsimile of contests past and limber up as if waiting instruction. He is quiet this time and from it I infer some respect, but I don't kid myself that will mean anything more than some caution and more ruthlessness.

CHAPTER 19

We square off and I find myself strangely detached from the outcome, and there is a release in the indifference. I take a deep breath and shuffle forward bobbing and weaving towards a static Marcus. He stands stoically in stance, left arm floating out in front, right hand loaded at the side, his hips twitching. I am setting to jab when the left foot leaves the ground and lashes diagonally upwards, scudding off my right shoulder as it rolls to the left. Marcus hops back to balance and his back foot buckles under the injury. I push off after him as he gathers his feet, shooting out the left jab and doubling it up when the first falls short. The second jab hits the cheek marking the range to fire the right hand. Primed and ready I let it go straight down the pipe towards his chin. He pulls back and it detonates in mid-air.

Switching direction, he launches forward throwing right and left fists like pistons at my head. I slip the first but the left stings the corner of my left eye, but I now have him where I want him - in a firefight. With my chin down I hurl a left hook and it glances the side of his nose. He pumps out another arrow straight right that bounces off the top of my head and stepping in skims the side of my face with an upward cutting elbow strike. I dip my legs and losing myself to a barbaric poetry let my hands go: ripping a right hook into his side and digging into his liver with a heavy left hook. Transferring weight through the hips I rattle his jaw with a short right cross then club him just below the ear with a left hook, that is slightly stray of where it needed to be to put him over. Bent legged and clutching his right side he steps backwards leaning at the waist as if to be sick.

I surge forward for the finish, but I am interrupted by a spike stepping pain in my shin that slows me right down. Marcus takes advantage of the reprieve and I see eagerness in his left leg. I duck to the left to avoid the kick and I am cleverly brought onto a front snap kick from the right foot. I take a brain juddering boot in the face that mashes lips against teeth; my eyes fuzz and I experience a tipping feeling like a tree being felled. I hear a gasp and the strike has hurt both ways, though it is an unequal trade. I fire back on instinct with a whistling left hook that wheels me with the miss a few feet over.

I could always take a drubbing and my head clears quickly. I rally my legs and prepare for an onslaught, blood the taste of iron in my mouth; and with a face a map of turmoil Marcus tears into me. From a southpaw stance I am caught on the cheek with a left reverse punch and it smarts instead of shakes. With a cross guard in place I continue to weave side to side but don't duck for danger of a knee. I have two weapons - well sometimes three when I elect to use my head. He has eight; but I have to take solace that my two are better than any of his two – I just had to connect cleanly and land one bomb before being hammered with another kick.

He doesn't come back in but follows the momentum of the punch to perform a roundhouse kick with the left foot. It is rising when I spring forward and thrust a ramrod left jab into the underside of his jaw. The impact cleans his clock and dumps him on his back. I am on him with an uppercut as he hastens up to his feet, the hurried blow cuffing his left ear.

Wild faced he grabs my shoulders and brings a knee into my stomach which I tense and take, though there is always a cost to be paid later in a long fight. He shoots another and I block it with a tucked elbow. Then with an open hand I twist and shove his left hand off my shoulder cocking the right hand for a hard, sapping hook to the ribs. I pull the fist in and angling my body drive it up through the middle as an uppercut. It makes solid contact with his chin, a fraction of a second before I feel I've walked into a post. In a moment the ringing subsides, the vision clears, and I see a nodding Marcus try to straighten up like a sozzled sailor before a gangplank. Blood flows immediately from my forehead in separate little streams dripping into, over and around my left eye. And I deduce that I've been sliced open by an elbow strike. I wipe away the blood, but it makes no difference, and it pours into my eye from its many tributaries.

Marcus breathing heavily puts hands on thighs and tries by head shaking to fix the focus of his eyes. Separated by seven yards I stare into his relatively unmarked face and grin, a big bloody, disfigured grin. He reciprocates and his teeth too are coated with blood.

Many a man had hate exorcised from him in the ring, and in its place a hard-earned respect grown in sweat, blood and grit. In another time or place, when the dust had settled I might have shaken his hand and bought him a drink.

I spit out a globule of blood, wipe my brow and get going. Marcus circles away, feinting attacks and creating angles, while I work my way in cutting off an imaginary ring, boxing him into nowhere. We are husks of what we were, damaged inside and out by now and before.

He smoothly changes to side on southpaw and with brutal skill and speed delivers a side stomp kick to my traumatized shin. The pain is excruciating, and I pull the leg away as though it had been put to a flame. This time he doesn't rush in, he circles and lets me hobble and bleed. It would seem the new tactic is to snipe with kicks at range, to pick at me like a matador would a bull; and damn if his fucking leg isn't hurt as bad I had thought. Not believing I could take another splintering stomp I leave my damaged leg behind and turn southy myself.

"You should see yourself bud, you're a fucking mess, you look like roadkill," he says with a red toothed smirk.
I am tired of listening to his bile, I had hoped that he'd shut up and now he's running off his mouth trash talking again. He's an on top shit talker so he must fancy the tide is turning in his favour. I have nothing smart to say or would I want to either. At this stage for me there is breath, blood and pain held together

with a violent intent - there is no space for words.

I advance watching the hips anticipating the kick to come. He switches over to orthodox sidling and suggesting an attack. I make up my mind not to wait and dive at him, unleashing with the dominant hand a crushing right jab with all my weight behind it. I angle off the centre line and get it outside his lead hand. It flies over the left shoulder, and the punch crashes into the side of his jaw, rapidly forcing the chin to the other shoulder. Marcus goes to sit like he's had a long day and is falling into his favourite chair. His head drops, he sinks back and a follow up shovel hook with the left hand smashes into the front of his face. Concussed and battered he collapses into a loose seat. I step back in love with my sore fists and count.

"One ... two ... three."

Marcus looks up, his top lip split, eyes in separate orbits.

"Four ... five," I count.

He pushes up to his knees as though he has suddenly aged forty years and gets in a position to stand.

"Six ... seven ... eight."

If he's not taking advantage of the count.

"Nine."

Marcus rises and I give him credit for being tough. It fitted with a preferred narrative that he'd be a cream puff bully that could dish it out and not take it, but this is not how it is.

"Beat your count," he says defiantly wearing a stupefied look.

He is unsteady and dazed though likely still dangerous as wounded animals are. His hands hover loutishly out in front and the stance is now squared and irregular. A kick from him would now put him over and a short salvo from me should put him away.

Marcus grins, shrugging off the hurt, boldly waving me in like it is all part of the plan. I line up the left hook and prepare to pull the trigger, when from behind the edge of a spade strikes down at his right shoulder. It hits the bony point with an unpleasant crack and the force drops Marcus to his knees. His face is frozen in surprise and he seems not to know where to look for an answer. Marcus's sick, shocked eyes ask me, then move to his hanging shoulder for an explanation, and finally understanding they look behind to accuse Toni.

Toni has both hands on the handle one on top of the other, and she leans on the spade as if she is taking a break from digging her allotment.

"That should to do it ... dislocated shoulder I reckon ... or maybe a fractured collarbone."

"Arrrgh you bitch! ... I fucking knew it ... aaaah," gasps Marcus.

Nursing his limp arm, he stands with a stagger, turning his back on me to face Toni.

"I had him, you spoiled it ... it was hard ... hard and fair and you ... you screwed it up! ... and took it away from me!"

Indignation had blown a fuse in my brain and I could hardly get the words out.

"It was too close Will, you were getting hurt ... and what was that shit with the count ... he wouldn't do that, he'd have shattered your face with the heel of his boot."

And she looks at me like I'm an oddity in a jar.

"We're not fucking playing here."

"But ... I had him," I repeat weakly realizing that I am right and wrong at the same time.

"I couldn't take the chance. There is more at stake here than your stupid, selfish pride. And besides he's hurt me more than anyone ... I deserved a piece, so quit the bitching."

I couldn't argue, I was seeking an ideal that had no place on this mountain, that had no currency with these people. I valued it, I knew it meant something, but is it putting value on fool's gold.

"Huh, I'm going to leave you two to it. Toni, I'm through, I'm done you've seen to that, I'm no threat now. I need to go to a hospital ... have it all."

Stooping and hugging his arm it takes effort for Marcus to speak as though he's pushing the words from his deathbed.

"That's very kind of you Marcus. You're no threat now it is true, but what about later back home, what then?"

"I'll leave you alone," he answers his lips hardly moving, his tone and mood muted and subdued.

"Nah, I don't see you or your sicko cousin doing that. After all you sent him down the basement to kill me."

Toni leans off the spade and readies its blade over her shoulder.

"He … he wasn't going to kill you … just scare you into keeping your mouth shut."

A mixture of pain and worry occupies Marcus's face and I realize that he is more scared of her than me.

"Right now, I could do it. I could swing this at your head and see what harm it did, and then do more of the same until all that remains is mush around a stump," Toni threatens manically, her lip curling mean at the end; yet I can see that it is fear that is at work behind the scenes.

"Okay Toni I didn't sign up for murder," I say trying to placate her.

"Think about it Toni, if you kill me, you've got to kill Martha and Adam too because they know I'm here … think now!" Let me walk away and go dig up whatever is there."

"Don't … wait!" shouts a female voice.

I turn and see Marta to my right with her hands raised in surrender walking down the mountain. As she gets nearer I see that she has the brooch in the palm of her right hand. I also notice that her jacket has a band of red tinged lining exposed along the left bicep.

"Let him go and I'll give you the brooch."

"Throw it over then," I say.

"Don't come too close Marta," warns Marcus.

Marta pitches the brooch at the optimum angle, and it travels a good distance, landing half a dozen yards in front of me.

"Go!" I tell Marcus.

Warily, keeping an eye on Toni, Marcus walks wearily towards Marta like a wounded soldier returning from the front line. Toni swears, harpoons the earth and kicks a tuft of grass. She places both hands on her hips and inhales and exhales vigorously enough that her nostrils flare.

"Come on let's get on it while I still got blood to bleed," I sullenly joke.

She strides over in a huff, holds my chin and says disapprovingly, "You'll live but you look more like a bulldog now. What was all that about?"

"Something I don't think you'd understand," I reply with a shrug of the shoulders and an overtone of regret – sympathy it seemed is frozen in the pipe.

"No, I don't, not any more I stopped doing stupid."

I'd been given both barrels, point blank range into the chest. I had no comebacks, nothing tart or pithy to say – I was stupid, am.

I pick up the brooch and know exhaustion is coming. An avalanche of it rumbling behind that will bury me sooner if I stop but will bury me all the same no matter what. I watch them climb up the peak, her stringy arm around his waist, helping him like a crutch. She had come back for him and that counted for a lot; it probably counted for more than anything else.

The cause of all this strife is a shiny silver circle the size of a coffee coaster with a rune engraved rim a quarter of an inch thick. Across the circumference from eight o'clock to three o'clock a silver thread the thickness of a match is shaped to form the curled peaks. Off the rim between four and five o'clock is a silver cord of exact thickness and about a half and inch long, culminating in a small amber cross. The brooch's rim is bevelled and has a simple hook type fastener at the back that would present the brooch to those who looked upon it as a picture. I sniff it and it smells of the crypt. I run my blood-stained fingers over its features and wonder if a little over a thousand years ago, a Viking called Gorm Longbeard had stood where I am now holding this brooch with blood on his hands too. Now people were willing to kill each other for the wish of gold that another had killed people for eras ago. And allow enough time to elapse, though perhaps not much time at all, and others succumbing to that base desire would set their hearts to do the same.

I drag myself over for the other spade, however Jon beats me to it and says in an avuncular sounding voice that would suit narration of a children's book,

"I got this young man, you guide us in."

Toni and Jon traipse up the slope to where Marcus left the detector. I hold the brooch up and manoeuvre to fit it to the mountain. I hang the picture on the twin peaks and the cross sits on the pair as they refine the spot with the detector. I shout up the slope,

"You're on it."

Conflict had held the cold at bay, but in its aftermath a frigid coastal wind devours me - my wet clothing a chilling second skin. In these conditions you are a missed step from grief and two from the grave. I head up the hill seeing Toni and Jon working in tandem shovelling earth; Toni oblivious to the cold digging with blind fervour. I cross over the ridge and retrieve our coats and gloves and catch sight of Marcus and Marta shambling back to a crippled car and a wall of despair – and know that when it rains it pours.

CHAPTER 20

By the time I return they are a couple of feet deep into the hillside. Toni has built a sweat and Jon has shorn his coat. Absent the baggy duffel Jon is a trim figure and with the vigour he attacks the earth seems unafflicted by the common, limiting ills of a man his age. He has a fleshy triangular nose between sunken, rheumy eyes and a weather-beaten complexion hedged by a full white beard, mottled in parts with grey; and although craning forward in a stoop stands taller than me by a good inch. With all that had gone on he hadn't said much. Those thin lips had parted with few words since I'd met him and it could be he isn't the talking type, or given the ensuing ugliness had nothing worth saying.

I make the mistake of stilly watching the cold brown dirt pile and the avalanche hits, engulfing me in exhaustion, calling me to the ground, pulling me into the dark reaches of surrender. Then the ding I hear revives my eyes.

"We've hit something!" exclaims Toni.

"Careful now," contrasts Jon his words unhurried and even.

They dig around widening the hole, cautiously excavating the clay like earth away from the sides of the tarnished object. I discern a circular lid and bowed sides.

"Different kind of *Workout of The Day*," says Toni grunting and working like a Navvy.

They beaver away, shovelling and scraping off the thick earth until the object is revealed to be a metal pot the size of a beer keg.

"Has one of you a phone with you?" asks Jon.

"They took mine," answers Toni.

"I have one," I reply.

"I need to take photos; can I use it?"

"Shouldn't you save the charge Will to navigate us back?" comments Toni attempting I sense to influence my answer.

"It's okay I know the way back," Jon assures.

I take out my phone and it has twenty-seven percent charge. I enter the swipe code, get the camera up and I hand it to him. Jon photographs the situation and then kneeling over gets a close-up shot of the pot. Jon then stands and beckons us to the hole.

"Stand in both of you. You are now famous treasure hunters and will be celebrated."

"No, no Jon the limelight is yours," replies Toni dismissing the idea.

"I don't understand ... er limelight."

"It means you can take the credit, I know how much it means to you; but first there needs to be something worth shouting about."

Jon holds the phone out with his left hand and with the right offers me a handshake.

"We haven't been properly introduced I'm Jon Einarsson and I am a friend of Toni's father Jim."

We shake hands, his grip is firm and warm from the digging.

"I'm William Cutter from South Wales and I've just got sucked into this," I say with a bewildered and busted smile on my chops.

"Well I'm glad you did William, I'm glad you did because it was looking bad for both of us. There is going to be a reward, and you'll get your share."

I turn and Toni is back working the spade.

CHAPTER 21

The pot is damn heavy in the tight hole and Jon suggests that we dig a trench to get at it. I have another idea and bending over the pot clean away the muck from the lid. I twist and pull, and it comes off easier than I imagine it would. Toni and Jon crowd around and we all see our fortunes change. Packed to the brim are gold coins, immaculate, glittering sovereignty of a bygone king. Hands collide and jam at the neck to grasp what is a dizzying and warping amount of gold.

"We've hit the fucking mother lode." exuberates Toni shaking me, glee blazing from her eyes.

"I knew it, I knew it ... they, the experts all laughed at me, ridiculed me for chasing a phantom ... now they will eat their words and give me my respect. Who will be the expert now, the giant ... hah?"

Bitterly euphoric and vengeful Jon had uncorked himself and what gushed out wasn't pretty. I understood where he was coming from; if I had walked in his shoes I'd want to rub their noses in it too - we all bore wounds from the slights and snubs of those whom we sought approval, and injustices from those we did and didn't. Before leaving I had been marinating in resentment and stockpiling grievances for a battle I couldn't yet fight; I had only hurt myself and I could now see myself in Jon.

Toni and I take turns scooping handfuls of gold coins out of the pot and onto the grass. Jon plucks just one and taking out a pair of spectacles from a breast pocket scrutinizes it.

"My, my ... is it?"

I stop to observe and see a man winning the lottery and incredulously staring at the ticket expecting the numbers to change. His thin lips tremble and he mouths incomplete words. He licks thin, cracked lips and utters,

"Ó Guð!"

Jon flaps, his synapses over stimulated with what is before him and what lay ahead. He checks the coin once more, then managing to harness the frenetic energy coursing through his body bustles over to the pile of coins. On his knees, he picks and examines, picks and examines, his face riffling with emotion.

"Ó Guð!"

"What is it Jon?" asks Toni.

"Will give me the phone," he says fidgeting like he's mainlined speed.

I open up my phone and hand it to him. I put my specs on and watch. Jon gets onto Google and enters *Syracuse Solidus* in the search bar. The first result is *Solidus of Irene, Syracuse – Historical Coin Market* and below are images similar to the coins I'd dug my fingers into. Gold pancaked into an imperfect circle with some a little ragged at the edges. They had been struck with a female monarch resplendent with robes, crown and cross topped sceptre. Jon brings the ancient and new together and it is though he can't trust his eyes as he compares. Jon scrolls down and clicks the link to the historical coin market, and I read the page with him.

Irene was a renowned beauty from Athens who became Empress Consort of the Byzantine Empire when she married Emperor Leo IV in 775 AD. After the death of Leo in 780 she assumed Regency on behalf of her son Constantine VI until 790, and then as the first Empress when Constantine died under mysterious circumstances. From 797 to 802 when she was deposed, she had coins minted in her likeness.

"*Solidus of Irene*, meaning a gold coin of Empress Irene in loros with cross potent in obverse, and in loros with globus cruciger in reverse. They were minted at Syracuse in Sicily between 797 and 802AD. The Roman Emperor Constantine started the Solidus and the Byzantines continued with them. For years I have chased Gorm Thorsen's Gold: where it is, how to find it and what it is? This is pretty much the best we could have hoped for."

"The Byzantines were the Eastern Roman Empire right? with a capital in Constantinople. How would it end up in Iceland?" I ask.

"My ancestors roamed far and wide raiding, trading and fighting as mercenaries. They sailed the Mediterranean and did one of those things to get it. And remember the coins had value outside of the empire in the rest of Europe ... so they could have come from elsewhere too!"

"What are they worth Jon?" says Toni keenly.

Jon kicks his head back and with a hearty laugh answers,

"Hah, the only question worth asking if you are not a scholar. Each coin in good condition is worth a starting price at auction of six hundred thousand Krona and have sold for over a million Krona. There will of course be a reward from the Cultural Heritage Agency of Iceland, and it will be a tenth of the value of the find. We will have fame and money in our pockets."

I try to do the conversion to pounds, but my tired and abused brain isn't up to it. I see Toni frowned in thought and surmise she is grappling with a similar calculation to dollars.

"Jeez that's about nine thousand dollars per coin," she announces with delight.

"Bloody hell!" I blurt and the thought of over a million dollars grips that tired, confused brain.

"Yes, so about three hundred dollars a coin each from the reward," says Jon with satisfaction.

We lighten the pot significantly so that I am able by hooking my hands inside to deadlift the pot out of the hole. We tip out the rest of the coins, and thrilled count the hoard like bandits - bandits with a foreboding of ill-gotten gains.

I pile the coins into stacks of ten and as I do so my disquiet grows. Toni had misread Jon. Jon wants glory not riches, he wants vindication and the accolades of academics. There would be a reward, but this is incidental and not the driver of his actions. Toni sees a staggering heap of dollar signs and a way out of the daily grind. Yet, she had not contradicted Jon and made an argument for keeping the gold.

I count the ten-piece stacks and there are sixty-two of them and four coins spare. I work the math on a calculator app, and I make it five million six hundred and sixteen thousand dollars at near the top value. I take a nought off and divide by three, and the cut rounded down is a clean, legitimate one hundred and eighty-seven thousand dollars. No further violence, subterfuge or shady deals, no rip-offs, police stings or looking over your shoulder. It is less, but could it be more?

Jon borrows my phone again and takes some shots of the pot next to the little pillars of gold. Then going down on one knee inserts himself in the picture as a fisherman would his catch.

"Will, a video please for proof and posterity."

I oblige and a more composed Jon provides us and a nation with a speech.

CHAPTER 22

We divide the weight of the coins by the strength to carry them. Jon knots the cuffs of his coat and packs coins into the sleeves. He then puts more onto the back of the coat and rolls it up into a bundle. Toni and I load all our pockets and refill the pot. We each hook a hand inside the pot and drag it the seventy yards to the shoulder of the mountain. I am as tired as an old pit pony, and I mark short distances and hirple my way to each, slogging past them one at a time. I can tell the others are flagging too, each of us silent with our own cross to bear.

The weather is changing for the worse. Clouds blacken and glower down and a mean wind harasses from the shore. We pick up the pace trying to outrun the gathering storm and the pot bumps over the ground behind us. We make our way across the rim over to the ridge the other side. I search for the Mitsubishi and it has gone, but do not assume the obvious. We descend the sheep track and I keep my eyes peeled and my wits about me. Taking my eyes off the ground in front of me I pay the price when a stone moves underfoot. I trip off the track and go over onto my left side, wheeling off the shoulder, legs in the air coming up sitting and sliding down the steep bank. Gaining momentum, I begin to tumble but before losing to it, turn over onto my front and claw the grass. Spreading wide, hugging and clutching the mountain I brake to a stop. I look up and Jon having set the bundle down steps off the track, while Toni still on the track tackles and steadies the rolling pot. With the pot braced against her shoulder Toni calls out,

"Will are you alright?"

"Just another one of my nine lives gone that's all," seeing that twenty feet further is the edge to a sharp drop.

I get to my feet with the same care a last card is placed in a house of cards. Using hands as well as feet I clamber back to the sheep track, pick up the spade and we continue down without further mishap.

At the bottom Jon needs to rest and Toni suggests going ahead for the car. It would be easier to not have to lug the gold any further, but splitting the party up weakened us as a unit. They seemed like they'd thrown in the towel, though five million dollars could assuage a ton of hurt. Because if you'd be prepared to do harm for the potential of it, what would you do for the promise? In the end it is the weather that decides. Day becomes dusk and fat raindrops pelt us like skirmishing fire for the barrage to come. I throw Toni the Ranger keys and Jon and I take shelter in the base of the bolt rock. The rain comes off the Fjord and with our backs to the rock we are spared the brunt of the downpour. In two minutes, the Ranger growls through the pass and assaulted by the rain we load her up.

CHAPTER 23

Jon has to take a leak before driving, and Toni chooses to sit in the back with me. She nestles into my shoulder and squeezes my hand. She whispers soothingly,

"I'm sorry I was hard on you."

"I deserved it."

"No ... well perhaps a bit. I just didn't like seeing you get hurt, taking unnecessary risks. I'm fond of you Will Cutter."

Even an apology from this woman is seductive and I am sure she could add sex to anything.

"It was reckless I know that, but I needed it."

"Needed what?" she asks.

I expel a lung full of air and feel the slow beating of my heart as I pause some seconds before breathing again.

"To fight and suffer, to suffer and fight, to go into the fire and come out ... or not," and as I speak the words I don't know whether to smile or cry, and it ends up being something in between.

"Wow, and I thought I had problems; it sounds like you don't care whether you live or die."

"Ambivalent, if I go I go."

"Well I want you to stick around," and I feel her hot breath in my ear.

She disentangles her hand from mine and slides it over my thigh to my groin. She rubs and cups my cock while her tongue dances wickedly in my ear. Arousal jolts me out of fatigue, I tingle, and the tempo of my heart quickens, and I am left chasing breath.

"Later, I'm going to give you all you can handle."

"I believe it."

I'd heard threats made softer.

Jon returns to the car and climbs into the driver's seat and says jest fully,

"What have you two love birds been up to?"

I laugh with faint embarrassment and see the ghost of my youth smooching in the front room with Beth, her parents in the next room with only frosted glass doors in between.

Jon slaps the wheel and exhorts,

"We're out of the storm guys and are homeward bound!"

And putting the Ranger into gear we trundle off through the rain the way we came.

For several minutes it hammers down, and the wipers can barely cope with the deluge. Jon though knows the route and the vehicle, and despite the atrocious conditions the Ranger advances along the crude, obscured road to Pingeyri. Here hunger and thirst join exhaustion. Emptiness gnaws and I feel as dry as a strip of jerky.

"Jon I could eat a horse and have a powerful thirst; can we stop quickly at the gas station so I can get something?"

"Sure, I'd say we could stop at the Simbahollin Cafe for coffee and waffles, but the windows are small, and you can't see the cars outside."

We enter Pingeyri and take a left soon after to the harbour.

"If you are ever here again that's Simbahollin Cafe," and he points out of the front passenger window.

I look through a misty, rain spattered window at a quaint, corrugated pea green house with a grey roof. Outside are wooden chairs and benches and a green coach with tourists alighting from it – and it creates cause to think that three days ago I was one of those innocent souls, well at least innocent of this.

Behind in juxtaposition is the utilitarian gas station with the red framed windows. It is a plain rectangular design composed of short white panels at the bottom, large windows in the middle and white facia along the flat roof line. Jon parks on the forecourt in front of the windows and I exit into the weakening rain, feeling like I am brittle and could break. The others too move with the speed of sloths, all of us nearly spent.

Jon locks the car and checks all the handles and we make our way to the entrance. Trade is slow and we have no bother slipping into a window booth. Jon sits one side and Toni and I the other. We order hot dogs and coffee and in the wait our beady eyes guard the car. Jon calls the waitress back over and speaks to her in Icelandic; then out of politeness discloses what he said, "Checking what they're cooking the hot dogs in; I've got a severe nut allergy and it has nearly killed me a couple of times."

"Yeah I remember Dad telling me about it after reading one of your letters. Told me that you had been rushed to hospital because your airway had almost closed," adds Toni.

"I've got EpiPens now, keep them in my medicine cabinet and I usually carry one with me." He laughs, "Not today though I was made to leave the house in a bit of a hurry."

Jon excuses himself, and before he has gone through the toilet doors, Toni flitting her pale blues between the car and me says softly,

"What do you think?"

"About what?"

"Handing the gold over," she says inviting conspiracy.

"Well there is a reward, it is a substantial amount of money and it is clean money," I reply.

"I've been mulling it over and I don't think we're going to get top price. This agency or whoever will put a conservative value on the gold. They already own it in law, it's government money, they will pay bottom dollar for sure. We'll be lucky to walk away with fifty thou apiece," she remarks sourly.

"Still a lot of money, Toni."

"You think so; is that the sum of your ambition Will Cutter, fifty thousand dollars?" and the kinked lips sneer in disappointment. It was the verbal equivalent of a liver punch and it robbed me of a reply. I take a moment,

"But ... wouldn't it be enough to clear your debts?"

"I want more for us than that Will. I don't just want to get my head above the water I want to get out of the water altogether."

"But what about Jon Toni? he's dead set on being a national hero. You got him completely wrong. He yearns for validation, to put right those people who wrote him off as a crank all these years. He is not going to take the gold and run."

She shakes her head, her mouth open in annoyance at me for not being tuned to her wavelength.

"He's an old man, he doesn't need money, he's after a swan song before the lights go out. It's our gold too and we have our lives ahead of us. You could quit the police, I could leave North Tonawanda, Marcus and Adam, and we could start a new life somewhere together."

Her hand grips my thigh and her ice blue eyes are searching, penetrating, demanding. I have a flush of unease and the arrow of my moral compass wavers much like it did outside the Leifur Eiriksson. The arrow moves and I am deviating off course. I allow myself to drift and I imagine a bespoke wooden house on a hill, or a beautiful beach house somewhere on Cape Cod. Then I envisage what I would have to do, what I would become, and I want no part of it.

"No Toni, we stick with the plan and we get what we get. I'm not going to steal or cheat the old man out of his share, or his day in the sun. I've been straight my whole life and I'm not breaking bad now."

"A fan?"

"From the outset, no jumping on the hype train here."

"And I bet you rooted for Walter throughout didn't you?"

"Yeah ... I did, but it's just a TV show."

"You like the bad guys, you just haven't got the balls to be one."

I could feel myself coming to the boil.

"Like Marcus, yeah? You listen to me I've risked my life to save your ungrateful ass. Not once, not twice, three fucking times. Don't you dare talk about balls to me; you know Toni your exposing a side of yourself that I don't care for, in fact I've detested in others. I think those cold, blue eyes only see dollars."

She takes it with little affect, her hide thick and inured to scathing words and ugly rows. Marcus could pierce it, but it appeared I carried too little weight with her to matter. She nods in that insolent way that marks a grievance, shifts over on the seat and looks away.

I had raised my voice more than I would have liked and attracted a few curious looks. I am glad to see Jon amble back to the booth. Before sitting down, he says chirpily,

"Still there then."

"Yeah for now," I sarcastically joke.

"Those thieves Will, do you think will come back?" and the chirpiness turns to concern.

"No, I don't think so, they're too busted up."

The hot dogs and coffee arrive and are wanted for more than their refreshment. I eat and drink with gusto, savouring the wholesome tastes and aromas. I welcome the relative silence and hope that a line has been drawn under Gorm's bloody gold.

I am finishing my second coffee when Toni asks grudgingly,

"Will I want to phone my father and see how he's doing. Can I use your phone?"

I pull out the phone, swipe across the dots and hand it to her. She gives the briefest of smiles - one no doubt drawn from her passive aggressive armoury and she tramps outside. I watch her with phone to ear pace the forecourt in sentry lines.

"You're sweet on her," says Jon in his kind storyteller's voice.

"More like stupid; when are you going to call it in?"

Jon looks at the hands of his wrist watch,

"Well it's close to three thirty and the department shuts at five. I'd like to get back, clean up and prepare my notes; get a good night's sleep and report the find when the office opens at nine tomorrow."

Toni with her face glistening wet comes back and places my phone on the table. She brushes a veiny hand through dripping hair, slicking it back to look like Carrie Anne Moss out of the Matrix, and I notice the coal black polish on her fingernails has chipped away.

"How is Jim?" asks Jon.

"Not so good," Toni replies tersely.

We pay up and walk out into the drizzle. Toni hangs back and I hear her say,

"I'll be a minute I'm getting some gum."

I stand at the car and watch the mist roll and coil on the mountains across the fjord. Inside my head is a jumble of thoughts swirling like leaves caught up in an autumn gust. There is here, there is home and what is left of me. I needed to hold onto something. And that while I could still see it is doing the right thing. Right has become a little blurred, but wrong is still clear enough. I decide to send Gudjohnsen a text informing him that I had found Toni and that she is fit and well. I keep the text brief and skimp on the detail. The police wouldn't be satisfied until they sighted her, but it would give them something. I finish by saying that we would report to Isafjordur Police Station tomorrow.

Jon gets in and I join him in the front. I plug my phone's USB cable into the charging port, to put life into a device that has been indispensable. A couple of minutes later Toni while unwrapping a stick of gum saunters over and slides in the back. She leans to the gap between the seats and puts her arm through, waggles the packet of gum in her hand and says,

"Any takers?"

Jon and I take a piece of gum and we roll out of the forecourt and join the road to Isafjordur.

Toni curls up on the back seat and goes out like a light. The heaters cook the cabin, and nicely full I too fall in and out of a nodding, disassociating sleep. I push my eyes open when hearing Jon exclaim,

"Wakey, wakey we're back in Isafjordur."

I stretch and rub them to back to life, and we are cruising along the inlet road towards the hook and Jon's house.

Jon slots the Ranger in the space in front of the house where it had been before. I get out, open the boot and retrieve the spade for what I desire to be the final time. I climb the steps to a building that has been a battleground. I inspect the windows and they are vacant. I hop over the drainage cover and go wide at the corners. The garden trees are still and damp in the dying light, and as night draws in the cold sharpens its knives. Toni is behind me with the axe held in concealment under the breast of an open coat.

"We get what we get," she says in a soft conciliatory tone.

I nod and push open the back door. The tiled kitchen floor is bereft of muddy footprints and I see no other signs that they have returned. We clear a room at a time and satisfied we are the only occupants I sling the spade into the earth. I then return to a swivel headed Jon who has locked himself in the Ranger with the engine running. We load ourselves with gold and make trips up and down the steps. In the kitchen we fill the silver pot, which in itself is a prize find and place the lid back on the top.

Then the three of us stand for moment staring at it lost in transformative thought. I have the least involvement, the least stake in this. I am an accidental tourist that swam into a maelstrom. One dormant for a thousand years and set back into motion by Jon, Toni, Marcus, Adam, Marta and me - all pulled into it, colliding and smashing into one another. I wedge the kitchen table against the back door and say,

"I don't know about you guys, but I could do with a drink."

CHAPTER 24

Jon goes into a corner of the lounge and opens a drinks cabinet that looks like a box made out of old, distressed floorboards. He lifts out a clear wine shaped bottle with a black label and places it on top of the cabinet. Then with his piano player's fingers he presses three shot glasses together and puts them alongside the bottle.

"This is Brennivin Iceland's own liquor, also known as *Svarti Dauði – Black Death*."

"I'll have a go at that," I offer, and taking one of the glasses hold it out in readiness.

Jon unscrews the cap and pours a full measure.

"What is the expression ... you are not backward at coming forward," he opines.

"It has been said," I reply.

When the other two are filled Jon raises his glass to us and offers a cheer,

"Skál."

Repeating the toast, I knock it back and it tastes pleasingly like licorice schnapps. Jon refills our glasses and with a quiver in his voice says,

"I pursued this dream, and it seemed like a dream for ten years. This means so much to me and I want to thank you for making it happen, and of course you will get an ample reward from the Heritage Agency for your troubles."

The glass is raised again, and I quaff another down, the thrusters firing, the dog let off its leash.

"Jon that is bloody nice," I hint wagging the glass.

Jon being a good host indulges my appetite and I not wanting to be too rude, take my time with the third.

Toni is first in the shower. I take a seat in a tired, old chair by the window, its red colour faded by the light, its firmness yielded a long time ago. Under the window there is a wooden chest that serves as a coffee table. On top of the tarnished wood is a runic metal coaster, a pair of round framed reading glasses and a book: *Egil's Sagas*. I sup some Black Death and think about the Nadurra I'm going to visit after it.

Jon kneels at the grate of a wood burning stove and constructs a pyramid of paper and kindling wood. He strikes a long match and nurtures a fire. The stove door is closed, the vents are opened up and the fire blazes to life. Jon adds more kindling and then a cut log from a half full basket at the side of the grate. He places the log carefully not to smother the fire and closes the door. It takes a minute for the fire to get its teeth into the log but once it does it ravages it with flames.

Wood crackles and the fire glows into the room. Jon sits in a sunken two-seater across from me.

"So, Will what do you think of Iceland?"

The joke is not missed, and I reply smiling,

"Well I think my tourist experience has certainly been different!"

"You've adventured like a Viking," says Jon chuckling and he raises his glass.

"I suppose I've always been an adventurer of sorts – a backyard adventurer in the sordid underbelly of life," I elaborate, knowingly straying into pretension for the fun of it,

"As a policeman I've never had to travel far to find trouble or for trouble to find me."

Jon nods and I can see the concentration of him qualifying the words.

"A policeman's lot is not a happy one."

It sounded familiar but from god knows where,

"That is from?"

"It's a song from The Pirates of Penzance. As well as Icelandic history I like musicals."

I cannot make my drink last any longer and finish it. I exaggerate the motion of placing the empty glass on the coaster. Jon takes the crude hint and fetches the bottle over,

"Another," he asks.

"Why not."

For there were few things worse than an uncertain or dwindling supply of booze.

"How well do you know Toni Jon?" I ask nestling the back of my head and shoulders into the chair.

"I have known of her all her life. I had met her father Jim before she was born. I've gone over to the States and visited Jim and his family a couple of times. The first time in 1990 and the last time in 1997. Toni wasn't there the second time she had dropped out of college and ran off to Miami with some party man. Jim and Joan were really pissed," and it is evident from the twinkle in his eye that Jon enjoys American vernacular too.

"Party man?" I query.

"Yeah … eh events, puts together events, music, dancing you understand?" explains Jon conjuring meaning with his hands.

"Ah an event organizer … yeah I know. So, she wasn't a dancer in New York then?"

"No, that was her sister Olivia I'm sure, and she now has her own dance studio in Boston."

The liquor is now talking and Jon dropping his voice says humorously,

"I think Toni, Toni is … the black sheep of the family."

Another lie, a segment of her sister's life stolen and used; what at all is true about her past?

Toni comes in rubbing her hair with a towel. She is wearing purple silk pyjamas and backless slippers. The nipples of her potent breasts are erect, and they push through the thin material. The sight sabotages my line of thinking and is a reminder to me of the weakness of men.

"I'm running you a hot bath Will and I've added some salts to ease your aches."

I'm split about confronting her, the accusation is poised on my tongue, but I choose to swallow it. This isn't the right time, perhaps there doesn't need to be a time at all? Just hand the gold over and go our separate ways. If it is that simple; it is the hooks that make it hard, they're in deep and there are pangs of hell knows what as I try to twist them free.

I hear splashing of water as I trudge up the stairs and see steam condensing against the glass at the top of the bathroom door. Along the landing I enter the bedroom of a long-departed son, where I will be laying down my head tonight. I sit on the side of the bed and flashback to the ennui of a week ago. It is still there, diminished by the danger of recent days, its spurs rubbed back for now. Numbed and cushioned by the alcohol to a tap that drips. I strip off my dirty, bloody, sweat odoured clothes and take the towel left for me by Toni.

The bathroom is decorated with sea green ceramic tiles that run dark on the floor and lighten up the walls. Subtly depicted waves roll along the edge with the odd dolphin and gull in and above them. There is the smell of salts and I pick up the aroma of lavender. I add enough cold to make the water tolerable and I lower myself in. The heat soothes and within a couple of minutes I feel the tug of sleep. Out of a pseudo politeness Toni knocks the door though doesn't wait for a reply. She shimmies in with a tumbler of whisky in each hand, the pyjama top open down to her navel and her lips in a filthy pout.

"A Nadurra for my hard-working boy," she purrs, the silk draping perilously around the half-moons of her breasts. She puts one tumbler into my hand and takes a sip from the other. Then leaning over she runs her left hand through my hair and clasping the back of my head plants a tender kiss on wounded lips. I taste the Nadurra and I think that there can't be anything better than a hot woman with whisky on her breath. She straightens up and the silk on the left side slips away revealing a firm, heavy breast with just the right amount of droop to make the artificial seem real. The bathroom light shines off the gold bar piercing, making it appear as a sun above the stark black tree below.

"You are right, I am wrong, it will work out though," she admits, her tone contrite yet sensuously coated.

I am disarmed and words rush out of my mouth to forgive.

"It's an insane, life changing amount of money Toni, capable of turning anyone's head. It had me for a minute … they don't call it gold fever for nothing."

She winks at the door,

"I'm going back to the fire, I'll see you in a bit."

I hunker down in the hot water and savour the Nadurra, and with its subtle notes prefer it to the Brennivin. I am in a pensive mood though I don't wish to be; I'd like to remove my head and put a blank one on instead - one that weighed a feather. But wishing don't make it so and I have to figure out what I'm going to do with my life. Firstly, I'd give Toni a pass on the lies. It could be she feels she needs to paint over a wasted, dissolute youth bumming around the clubs of Miami – then who am I to puncture that balloon - I too had sold myself short.

Secondly, what of work: I would go back and fight, fight the complaint and fight to get back out on the street where I belonged. I would not give the smug, brown nosing ladder climber the satisfaction of feeding me to the wolves. I would cut down on the booze, get running again, coach at the club, and just try to see straight – it is what Beth would want. And Antonia Brookes, well the whirlwind had to subside to find out if there is anything the other side of it. If there is something it would survive and be built upon in one of those sad long-distance relationships that Marcus frowned upon. Take a step back, uncloud my judgement and carefully strip back the lies - maybe, then maybe.

I grin that I may have found my way back to the path and reach for my phone to call Nathan for a quick chat. I press the phone icon and the call log appears. The last call is the one Toni made to her father. I look at the mobile phone number and a sudden stabbing suspicion moves me to check it. I enter the number into Google and search for it first. It pops up, and although I'm not completely shocked at the result, a sickening anger ignites in me. The number is listed under K.B. Aviation and I learn from visiting the website that K.B. is Kyle Banks, a commercial pilot based out of Albany, New York.

Kyle has his own plane - a red and white Cessna 210 Centurion, and K.B. Aviation offers a number of aerial services, though smuggling gold coins internationally doesn't seem to be one of them. K.B. has a photograph of himself above a resume that I haven't the time to read.

He is a plain, chinless man approaching fifty with the indolent body you get from sitting down all your working life. K.B. hadn't stood a chance with Toni, he wouldn't have known what hit him - she would have knocked him clean out of the park. I imprint his face and file it to memory. I take a gulp of Nadurra and give Kyle a bell. He answers on the fourth ring and carelessly speaks first, offloading information,

"Babe, I'm on my way, I've hired a car, booked a motel and the plane is being refuelled at Bildudalur for an 8am flight. I should be with you in twenty minutes - I can't wait to see you. Is everything going according to plan?" He speaks rapidly, nervously and with a thick, whiny, New York accent.

"Babe are you there?" his voice rising an octave.

I cut him dead and make a quick note of the destination and registration number of the plane - N771DH. A plan is under way and I have a part, a part I don't know, a part that I fear I'm not going to like.

I climb out of the bath and feel light headed. I half dry off and still wet go into the bedroom. I still feel dizzy and the wall zooms in and out. I'd shipped a few hard shots to the head over the last couple of days, had slept poorly and been hitting the

bottle pretty hard – I needed to slow down and rest up. I dress quickly and putting on my boots I roll off the bed. No, I could take a beating and hold my booze – this is something else. I lay there feeling smothered by fatigue and with the room moving around, it dawns on me that I've been drugged.

I crawl to the door and use the frame to pull myself up. I use the wall to keep me upright and cling onto the bannister for dear life. I am walking on pillows and my knees seem to have been replaced by worn springs. I'm in shit shape and need help. I fumble for my phone to call the police, patting and scooping pockets for a phone that I'd left in the bathroom. I turn on the stairs to go back up and get it and the toe of my boot scrapes the carpet and extends through. I fall on my front and slide down to the bottom. I push up, lose my balance and giddy as a spun drunk career off the doorway of the study, stumble over and sprawl onto the hardwood floor.

Lying face down my body acts like it is encased in rusty armour and could sink right through the floor into unknown depths beneath. With great effort I prop myself up into a frog squat and topple on to my ass. I vaguely hear a click, and a distortion of it in echo, though I am unable to detect the direction or distance of the sound. I see the lounge door in front of me open, and Jon is standing the other side, not looking well at all.

CHAPTER 25

Jon's face is grotesquely swollen, his skin is blotchy, and his eyes are puffed out to slits. He wheezes through sausage fat lips that seem ready to burst, and his engorged throat is one you would see on a bed bound glutton. Toni swoops from behind, wraps her right arm around his shoulder like a cape and whisks him back into the room. I hear Toni, her voice tinny and dislocated.

"When they broke in they must have disconnected the phone and hid it somewhere!"

I crawl to the door and pull myself up the frame. Jon has been seated and is crouched over his knees. The wheezing is loud and whistling and the bloated lips are cyanosis blue. Toni stands cross armed on the threshold of the living room and kitchen. Behind her an open cupboard door its contents in disarray, ransacked onto the kitchen counter and floor.

"Hold tight Jon, I'll carry on searching for an EpiPen," she says calmly in a voice that is nearly monotone.

The room spins slowly, stops and zooms in and out. Objects fuzz and blur and then the floor moves like the drop dive of a roller coaster. I cling onto the door frame with arms made of lead and look to my left to the front door. I have to get out of the house. A hand grips my chin and twists it back. Her face is in front of mine and she says flatly without expression,

"Will you are howling drunk, you'd better lie down."

"Yoo ... Yoou druug."

"Yes Will, I put GHB in your whisky; we get what we get you

said, how true. Now sit down!"

She bares her teeth and shoves my head back and I fall heavily to the floor. I raise myself onto an elbow and Jon is off the chair and on all fours. I hear with varying volume and effect his desperate, strangulated wheezing, then the strength in the arms gives out and he is forehead to the floor drawing his final constricted breaths. She gazes down on me with her hands on her hips, no more the sultry gunfighter - just a killer.

"It is always said Will that women are good at multitasking, well I guess this is proof of it," and she scoffs cruelly.

I struggle to get up, but all of gravity is against me and I collapse on my back. The hallway light dives and rises, dives and rises. The shape of her stands over me, hazed and vibrating, cold blue fire flashing from her eyes.

"It is a shame you were too much of a pig. It was an asset in the beginning, but an obstacle at the end. Go to sleep Will and the dreadfulness will soon be nothing."

Her voice is in stereo, distant, loud, resonant and at times garbled and hoarsely satanic. Shadows sprout from her back, flapping and spasming into terrors like a dozen raven's wings. My eyes flicker, and it seems that I am ceasing to breathe, and then the darkness comes.

CHAPTER 26

A sound pierces my unconsciousness and I assimilate it into a dark, torpid dream. The sound persists and cracks open the dream. I am jolted awake, yanked from the realms of the dead by *Get Carter.* My eyes blur into focus as the phone throbs the tune. The screen illuminates the pine needle earth on which it rests; a candle in a canopy of thick night. In attempting to sit up I am braked by something I have around my neck. Instinctively I reach for my throat and icicle cold fingers touch the coarse fabric of a towel. The towel is densely rolled and fixed in a tight noose with the knot at the nape of the neck. I loosen it like I would a tie, then I twist at the waist and rotate round until I can reach the phone without rising.

I think it is Annabel and I swipe towards the green phone icon to answer.

"Dad, Dad is that you, are you all right? Please don't do anything silly please!" my daughter begs crying hysterically.

"Mam would never forgive you!"

"I'm okay, I'm okay what do you mean?" I slur, confused to what the hell had happened or what is happening now.

"The text Dad, the text you sent everyone saying that you'd had enough, that you couldn't live any longer without Beth, that you were sorry but had to end it."

I am lagging from whatever I'd been given, and my recollection of events is fragmented, yet I knew I wouldn't inflict that pain with a text of all bloody things. Keeping the phone to my ear I turn toward the knot and in the glow see a belt looped around the towel and buckled to a broken branch.

"No, I didn't Bell ... that wasn't me ... I wouldn't do that to you."

"What do you mean it wasn't you? Have you got blind drunk again, and sent a lot of shit that you don't remember sending?"

I loved my daughter's voice; however, anxiety and anger had made it a shrill sound to my hurting head. I feel like the slowest kid in the class who can't keep up, who stares out of the window daydreaming – adrift from it all.

"Something has happened Bell ... I'm not sure what yet. Just know that I'm okay and that I'm coming home. I got to go."

"No Dad ..."

"Listen! I'm fine I've got something to do then I'll call you I promise."

I terminate the call and tap the torch app. I examine my surroundings and I am in a clot of coniferous trees littered with pine needles. Downwards, several feet away at the base of a fir tree I spot my travel bag and coat heaped together. The tree I am next to is deciduous and has shed most of its leaves and only a few shrivelled ones remain to fall. I pull the towel from my neck and it is one that I had packed in my travel bag. The belt is mine and has been taken from my waist. The broken branch which the belt is looped around is as thick as a rolled-up newspaper. It is dry to the touch and on the verge of being rotten. It is a branch that given the choice you would not have used, however the fir trees offered little else for a ligature point. The stub which the branch has snapped from comes off the trunk of a skinny, grey tree, and is just over six feet off the ground. Considering the length of the belt, I work out that I would have hung partially suspended in a position between sitting and standing up.

I realize I hadn't done this myself. I had been drugged and brought here, strung up with my own belongings and left to die. If I had been religious I would have given thanks to a higher power, but I'm not so I don't. The truth of it is if the branch had been perhaps a fraction stronger I'd be dead. If they had taken me to another location I'd probably be dead. There is no miracle here, there is only bad judgement and dumb luck. I had hung not long enough to die, though long enough for them to think that I would before they left. It was a narrow ledge on which my life had been balanced, such a thin margin of seconds. How many forty, twenty, ten – I would never know except that death was decided in seconds, and sometimes their fractions. The equation made me livid.

I open the messages on my phone and on the way see the eight missed calls that I had received. I still have my glasses and I read what had been text.

To those I love I'm so sorry. I can't go on without Beth, my life is misery without her. I have to end it here and now. Sorry I love you all, Dad.

The message had been sent to Nathan and Annabel at 20:29 and it is now 04:41. Nathan hadn't responded to the text, so I send him a message that it had been sent by someone in spite. I send the same message to Annabel to offer some explanation for the suicide note.

I am as cold as the grave, and I lumber to my coat to put it on. The hanging had nearly killed me and now the cold is having a try. I would have to get indoors and get some warmth soon, but first I needed a few evidential photographs of this nice little scene: a fine set up, nothing alien, all contained, no sign of third-party involvement – neat. The directional arrows pointed to suicide; she had seen to that and the messages to love ones off a coded phone closed the book. I take a couple of wide, encompassing shots and a close-up of each individual component in the staged suicide.

I collect the towel, belt and bag, then using the torch on the phone stagger downwards through the thicket in hope that there is a road or something beyond. I get whipped in the face by scraggy branches before finding a track that leads abruptly out onto open hillside, and a panoramic view of Isafjordur at night. Below is the tightly lit scimitar shaped peninsula, and across the black simmering water the runway lights of the airport.

They hadn't bothered going far to dump me; I am no more than three hundred yards as the crow flies from the old man's house. Then a shard of memory like a piece of glass from a shattered bottle, whose fragments had been scattered is tread upon, and the memory enters like pain. Jon is swollen at the door. The image is vivid and by concentrating I hear him wheeze and see him crumble and suffocate in front of the fire. Accompanied by the thought I walk down the hill onto a road. The road I need to get to is the one below and huddling into my coat, with vapour billowing from my mouth into the frigid night air, I grind the yards.

I round the bend to the street and see headlights drawing near. I duck next to a parked car and the interior of the car is lit up by the passing beams. My heart convulses and nausea rises with a prickle of sweat. I vomit a soup like sick and the head pounds in unison with the heart. I cough and spit the acid leftovers from my throat and breathe deeply; my hands trembling from a cocktail of poisons. I walk to the house; the Ranger is in its space and a red Volvo that had been there before is next to it.

I get to the gate when another memory returns, and it is Toni sashaying in silk pyjamas, tantalising with curves and whisky. It turns my stomach how easily she pulled me in and played me out - dispensed callously like a loyal cart horse sent to the knacker's yard. But I reserve much of the ire for myself – I had been led, but when I had not been led I had stepped forward, indeed ran headlong.

An incandescent moon sears a hole through night's black mantle. Its fullness intrudes, looming over me like it is falling from the sky. The garden trees swish as I climb the steps and I take no care not to be seen, because in my bones I know them to be long gone. I'm here for Jon, in the slim chance that he is clinging onto a scrap of life. I enter through the damaged back door that will prove the sticking point in passing Jon's death off as misadventure. The table is back in place and the gold is gone. Jon is down on his knees with the left ear to the wooden floor as though he were trying to hear rats scurrying underneath the floorboards. I had found a heroin addict overdosed in the same position, belt wound around the bicep and needle still in the forearm.

The fire has burnt out to grey, white ash and a chill has returned to the room. I bend down to him, his face squashed into the floor, the blood migrating down, pooling into his compressed features. The hands waxy and lifeless cold are locked in rigor - I don't need to see any more.

I stand up and notice an empty tumbler on a side table next to the sunken chair, and maybe it is significant. The gruesome ballooning was anaphylactic shock and it had shut his airway and choked him dead. Jon was severely allergic to nuts, so how had Toni got Jon to consume something containing them? I don't have the answer, but I can point the police in the right direction. I'll tell them about the gold and how it turned murderous. I'll show them the photographs of the treasure; then it comes to me that Toni didn't want or have her picture taken and is not in the video. In hindsight you could put the pieces together, but what good is that when the treachery has occurred, and the blood has already been spilled.

I open the gallery of my phone and a stomach already off kilter dives. The photographs and video are gone, deleted, wiped from history. I nod with a grudging respect and sigh; assuming the expression I'd seen criminals make when they had reached the end of the line and had nowhere to go.

What did I have: a fanciful story, a busted door and a dead man on the floor that witnesses could say I had been looking for? Toni is in the wind, possibly a figment of my imagination or a scapegoat for guilty lies. Only Marcus, Adam and Marta, a line of scurrilous shitbags to back me up – I don't want to get caught in that crossfire.

I had to see it from a cop's perspective, if I am looking at it and it isn't me. I have diminishing credibility, I am someone on the slide, someone that would get into deep trouble, someone who you wouldn't blink an eye if they hung themselves. I can't take the chance with what I got, it could backfire badly - I've got to get proof. I go to the kitchen, to the rack and unhook the Ranger keys and return to the gnawing cold. I see the spade struck into the soil and pull it free – there is a job to be done, a reckoning to come.

CHAPTER 27

I search for further fragments of a nightmare and the ugly, unsettling pieces I don't need I find. I sift and pan the splintered, obfuscated memories knowing that there is a nugget of importance to be found. The clock in the Ranger reads 5:12, time is running out and it prompts the question why? Then from the bowels of my brain the answer surfaces - because they are flying out of the country in the morning. Then I remember the lavender bath and the phone conversation, and that I'd been smart enough to make a note.

Bildudalur Airport 8am, Cessna 210 Centurion N771DH Kyle Banks.

I pick up a can of Red Bull from the drinks holder and put the phone in its place. It is a two hour and thirty-eight minute drive along the blue line of the screen, passing through Pingeyri and then further south and west along another fjord. I crack open the Red Bull, start the engine and turn the heaters on full. I swing the Ranger out, drive cautiously to the limits of town and then press hard. The headlights at full beam push the dark away from a desolate road and I urge the Ranger on. Slowing just enough before the bends then surging through, riding the road and the edge of an impaired ability.

My head is clearer than when I took the phone call, though I feel worse. The sickness is the queasy, green about the gills variety you'd get if you sucked on an exhaust pipe; and I have to pull into a side track before Pingeyri to be sick. I bring up acrid bile, then retch next to nothing and my brain pulsates. I crawl back in the cab, beads of bad sweat rolling from brow to cheek and a loathing for her festers in my rotting gut. I vent it on the accelerator slamming it to the floor and zigzag back onto the road.

The bridge over the fjord is reached, and as it is crossed thoughts of the previous night's crossing perturb. Then I had been giddy on possibility, excited by discovery and eager to beat a fresh, new path. Now in the wreckage of that I am more jaded than ever.

In Pingeyri I turn left and head further south on the **Vestfjaroarvegur** into the hinterland and a single lane dirt road. And save for the faint witness of the moon now dampened behind sailing grey clouds, it is solitary and utmost dark, as black as her stone heart. The road winds, and is at times indistinct from the stony, barren terrain that surrounds.

It is a demanding drive and I am keyed into it, my right hand busy with the gears, the feet hot stepping the accelerator, brake and clutch. The road lowers into another fjord and I thunder down it, and then follow the road east around its bank. The dirt road then veers from the shore inland and south again. Sixty miles in and I hit a fork in the road and carve a fast right turn causing a storm of small stones to plink off the undercarriage. The car clock reads 7:06 and according to the map there is nearly another thirty miles to the airport.

Out of a bend our headlights lock and reducing speed I dip the beam. I pull off the road and resting on a slight tilt give way to the oncoming car. Cruising, slowly into the headlights I see the livery and emergency roof lights of a police patrol car. I had been on the opposite side of this situation countless times, scrutinizing a driver looking for giveaways and tells, waiting for my gut to speak. I would often just look and know, like an article of faith that the person behind the wheel was worth a pull and listening to my gut I'd take a punt. It was a gamble where if you weren't right you didn't lose, so I played fast and loose and some said I was lucky, but luck had nothing to do with it – you make your own luck, and I have the fear and hatred to prove it. Now the eyes are on me and I have something to hide. I am driving a murdered man's car and if they pull me and ask a couple of basic questions I'm stuffed.

The trick is not to give that away with furtive behaviour like shielding your face with your shoulder or rubbing your nose. I choose to give the cops eye contact, not too much to indicate hostility or over watchfulness, yet not too little to suggest avoidance and apprehension. I attempt to project the coolness of a man going about his daily business. So, I nod and smile to the cop driving, when he acknowledges with a wave my courtesy in letting him pass. The time played a part too. At this time of the morning they were probably the night shift coming back late from a shout. They'd have blinkers on with only bed on their minds.

I drive west and the road re-joins a jagged coastline overlooked by white, flat topped mountains, their sides bare and deeply grooved. I enter a narrow bay just before Bildudalur, the blue line short on the sat nav, the last direction a double back right turn on the other side. I glance at the digital clock and see the digits change to 07:50. There is ten minutes to take off. I know little about small aircraft; however, I estimate that this close to take off they'd have finished loading and prepping the plane and are probably on board.

Black has morphed to a bruised blue in twilight, and I see the runway like a jetty in the water running parallel to the road. I stop the car and grab the big lensed binoculars from the back seat.

The airport is unassuming and is crafted much like the one at Isafjordur, though more basic and provincial still. It has a modest blue and white building with a watchtower as a terminal. There is a rough car park with a Nissan Qashqai, and a silver SUV with a yellow light on the roof parked inside. Alongside the terminal there is a single strip runway with a staggered white line down the centre, and upon it a small red and white single propeller aircraft. The boarding steps are down and from behind the plane a figure emerges. He is a gawky looking man with narrow shoulders and wispy salt and pepper hair. He wears a red flight suit with zips, patches and neoprene seals - I make him to be Kyle. Kyle checks the wing and then climbs up the steps into the plane. A few seconds later Toni also wearing a red flight suit comes from behind the plane, however hers is only worn half on with the arms tied around the waist. She briefly looks up in my direction, her beautifully crooked face framed in the lens, and in this moment I burn to be viewing this image through the scope of my Tikka .204. Placing the crosshair on her forehead, setting the trigger, and with a soft squeeze sending a bullet to empty the awful contents of her head.

She hops up the steps onto the plane and I transform hostile thought into hostile action. I toss the binoculars onto the back seat, get up the dialler on the phone and hastily press 112. As it starts to ring I put the Ranger in gear and go. One eye on the road the other on the plane as it taxis along the runway. I drive to the acute turn and take a wide arc into the road. The call handler answers and in staccato I blurt,

"I am William Cutter at Bildudalur Airport, suspects in the murder of Jon Einarsson of twenty-two Hildevargur, Isafjordur, fleeing the country in a Cessna 210. On board valuable Viking artefacts, I am apprehending."

He says something but I have tuned out, occluding the extraneous my vision tunnelling to a gap between the terminal and runway's rocky edge. I shoot through the gap and straighten out onto the strip. I floor the accelerator and shifting through gears the needle rises. Ahead the plane reaches the end of the runaway and the Ranger hurtles towards it like a rocket - a rocket hell bent on destruction. I fix on the plane, the periphery of my vision streaming lines whooshing past. The plane manoeuvres into a take-off position exposing its flank and where I will spear it. Just over a hundred yards out I cut over half the speed, and as I close I lock eyes with their terror. Jaw clenched, gripping the wheel I brace myself for the impact.

In a cacophony of clashing metal, the Ranger rams into the undercarriage taking out the landing gear shoving the plane off the strip. The bonnet crumples, the windscreen fractures and I rock in the seat. The Cessna keels over onto the rocks, a wing impaled in the water holding the fuselage on the waterline. The Ranger halts a few feet from the edge with steam emanating from a broken radiator.

I unbuckle the seatbelt and force the door open, pull the spade from the back seat and stride the few steps to the rocky bank; the smell of battery acid and salty sea air in my nostrils. The cockpit door swings open and falls back on itself. It then flies open and hangs on its hinge. Two hands grip the frame of the door and like a baby chick straining to get out of its shell, Kyle gasping with red faced exertion inches himself out of the plane. Unable to steady himself he flops out like a fish hauled onto a ship's deck.

Stoked by vengeance the ills fade and thrown back ten years I skip over the rocks as I used to when running over hard terrain. He is getting up when I get to him. I seize a clump of hair and roughly drag him yelping and stumbling up the ragged, sharp volcanic rock. I lose the spade and release my right hand from his hair. He straightens up and his eyes are saucers of disbelief, and hands float up in front of a slack aghast mouth, open and placatory. Kyle is the proverbial deer in the headlights, frozen in front of a dead man standing. Gruffly, I spit,
"We haven't been properly introduced."

I whip a mean, jaw jarring left hook around an impotent defence and knock him over like a well struck skittle. I leave him sprawled out with his eyes rolled into the back of his head and his foot twitching. With the underling taken care of I return to the Cessna to deal with the queen. She is not traversing the rocks or clawing her way out of the plane. I scan the water and shore, then I run to each point and visually search along the sides of the strip - concluding she must still be in the Cessna.

The airport SUV with its amber light flashing is tearing along the runway. I hop across the rocks and the wing propping up the plane gives way and the fuselage drops below the waterline. I clamber on board and crawl towards the cockpit. The stinging cold sea laps over, and the plane an uncertain platform undulates with my weight. Peering inside I see Toni on her right side. Her head is craning above the water and she is trapped in her seat. The water is gushing in, enveloping her in an icy embrace and reaching for a forever kiss. She thrashes at the cross harness holding her in the seat. Strapped in a seat of execution, the cockpit the chamber and I presiding, passing sentence.

"Help me!" she gasps in the throes of panic, bucking against the restraint and ripping ineffectually at the release buckle with her left hand; the right arm seemingly stuck against her side. The worst of my nature would watch her drown for what she'd done, but I need her alive. The water is at her neck and I don't have long to save her. I remember the knife she had. The compact, black bladed lock knife that she produced from a pocket in that brown leather jacket.

I lower myself in and precariously balance with one foot on an armrest and the other on the dashboard. There is the sound of scraping metal and the plane lurches. I tense every muscle fibre holding position, aware that this could become my coffin too. "Your knife Toni, where is it?"

"Breast pocket," she pants, her breathing rapid and shallow, the cold water shock taking her.

The water now against her right ear and slicing across her chin. I brace off the roof and leaning down put a hand on her head rest to steady myself. I quell the sickness that she gave me and unzip the pocket. Shaking, I slip my hand in and carefully retrieve the lock knife. I put it between my teeth and step down over her, placing my foot on the submerged cockpit window. I feel the chill of the water as it seeps through my boot and circles my lower leg. The knife opens with a snap and with my left hand I grab a fistful of the belt and lift. The water rises, entering the corner of her mouth causing her to spit and splutter for breath. The knife slides under the space, and with a tugging and sawing motion it is cut. I hold up the shoulder straps and pull her from under them.

I hear a voice from outside and see a man in a lemon overall with grey reflective strips leaning over and looking in. The man is burly with a broad face and fair, crew cut hair. He has hooded eyes that make him look sleepy, or otherwise disinterested and a small turned up nose that sits incongruously with the rest of his face. He has a florid complexion and appears to be around thirty. He flattens against the doorway and extends a thick arm through, and with a raised voice barks "Quick, take my hand."

The aircraft groans and the sea pours in. I am squashing Toni in, so I must exit first. I clasp the meaty hand above me and use the tension in the arm to spring up onto the lip of the door. I get both hands on and heave myself out. I then mimic the crewman's position on the other side of the door so that two arms dangle into the cockpit.

It is impossible to separate the sheer horror of a creeping death inching towards you, from the distress of facing someone you believed you had murdered, and Toni's face is an amalgamation of alarm. She flinches from my outstretched arm and takes the crewman's hand. He lifts her part of the way up and then I grip her by the jacket, and we lift her half out. I switch grip to her belt and see the old nautical compass tattoo at the base of her back. It is beautiful piece of work, but a tramp stamp, nonetheless.

CHAPTER 28

Messily, we get down from the plane and ascend the rocks. The front doors of the grey Toyota Hilux are swung open and the amber light revolves and flashes in the dimness of the dawn. Another airport guy in a voluminous orange work coat with a phone in his hand is kneeling next to a still unconscious Kyle. The man pinching the phone between ear and shoulder rolls Kyle onto his side into the recovery position.
"You crash into the plane," states the crewman warily watching me, and the half-drowned rat jumps in,
"He tried to kill us, he's crazy!"
The guy in the open orange coat stands up and moves four o'clock to my position. Shortish and slim, he has a full head of black hair neatly combed in a side parting, is older than the crewman and underneath the coat is dressed more for management than maintenance. I'm not having any of it, I'll allow her no more twists and turns. Pointing, I channel the authority of twenty-three years of telling people how it is,
"This man, this woman have murdered Jon Einarsson in Isafjordur, attempted to murder me, and on that plane is stolen gold. I have stopped them leaving the country and you are to hold them until the police arrive. I have phoned the police and they are on their way."
"Lies! He is the criminal, you've just seen what he did with your own eyes," protests Toni shivering like a shitting dog, strands of wet hair stuck to the right side of her face like the oily, black tentacles of her Kraken tattoo.
"What I say is true. There is gold in that plane and a dead man

in Isafjordur named Jon Einarsson. These are facts that can be known," I declare with conviction.

"I don't know anything about a murdered man, but you do so perhaps you killed him," she responds rankled.

The crewman rubs the side of his face and runs the point of his tongue along the bottom lip. He is about to say something when I interrupt.

"The gold Toni, explain the five million dollars worth of Viking gold on your plane, explain it! You can't, or maybe you can, put the blame on Kyle here, get him to take the fall. Just another man scrunched up and tossed in the bin. You picked the wrong man for a stooge Toni, I'm taking you down, you cold blooded bitch."

In the distance I hear the long wail of a siren. I listen to it become louder and alternate to a rapid two tone. It is coming from the direction of Bildudalur the other side of the bay. The siren blares as the white police car rounds the promontory and drops off the coastal road into the airport. It speeds along the runway with spinning blue lights, then dramatically brakes to a skidding halt. Doors spring open and two male uniformed cops alight from the Volvo Crossover SUV. The driver is tall and blonde, lean and young with a face that could be described as pretty and somewhat feminine. The passenger is his opposite, worldly mid-thirties, average height, lantern jawed and densely muscled with a bearing that said he took no shit.

The hardnosed cop eyed everyone then gave an instruction in Icelandic. The fresh face cop responds and jogs over to the still stricken pilot. Kyle had been a sitting duck and the left hook vicious. I had wanted to knock him out, out cold over several ten counts; now it is looking like there could have been too much heat on that hook.

Hard Nose takes the centre and questions the airport crew in Icelandic. For a minute a conversation went back and forth and at the end Hard Nose says brusquely,

"What is your name?"

"William Cutter."

"You are reporting homicide?" he asks in a heavy accent of clipped English.

"Yes, last night that woman Antonia Brookes and that man Kyle Banks poisoned a man from Isafjordur called Jon Einarsson. His body is on the living room floor at twenty-two Hildevargur. They murdered him for the gold on that plane."

I listen to how I am talking my way into becoming a murder suspect, but there is no other way. I have got to keep digging that hole and hope I come out of the other side of it, because it is all too late now to climb back out.

I hear more sirens, a blend of two or more closing in. The airport man in the orange coat takes it off and drapes it over Toni's shoulders. She smiles at him, gorgeous to the unsuspecting, unyieldingly gorgeous still to those that should know better. Toni steps in front of Hard Nose lasering him with her cold blue eyes. Sassy, tough Toni disappears, and little girl lost Toni with an upset voice comes to the fore.

"He crashed into our plane, almost killed us. He's obsessed with me, he's a madman who's been stalking me since I got here."

Hard Nose breaks her gaze and looks down at the toe of his left boot like he's about to kick a penalty. He touches the earpiece and speaks into the radio on the jacket's lapel. Kyle wakes with a start on queer street, and with glazed over eyes groggily paws at some imaginary handle that he thinks will help him to his feet. Hard Nose sidesteps to align himself with a view of the Ranger's registration plate. I don't understand what he is saying over the radio but I know he's running the registration through a database. Another police patrol car followed by a red fire engine and a red and yellow lined ambulance drop onto the airport road and make their way across the strip.

Hard Nose says to me,

"I'm arresting you under article 165 for causing danger to the public and damage to property. I am also arresting you under article 211 on suspicion of taking the life of another person. You are being detained to prevent any further loss of life. I am handcuffing you, turn around and place your hands behind your back."

I comply, it was to be expected. He snaps the rigid handcuffs on, and the broadness of my shoulders pulls my wrists against the metal bracelets – it would be a long uncomfortable ride. He leads me to the Volvo and angling my head I see a touch of smugness on those lips. She catches herself and a smile is subdued to the better affectation of victimhood. The tears, the stunned, choking shock, the gentle collapse - and the rat slips down the drain. A paramedic tends to her, another Kyle, and I'm the bad guy being bent into the back of the Volvo. Confidence deserts me like a wronged man, a condemned man being moved to his place in the tale. I rail against the shadow of the noose,

"Detain them too, there are stolen gold coins on that plane, which they killed Jon Einarsson for. I can prove it, don't let them go."

Stern and stoic like the mountains he seems indifferent. I shift in the seat to alleviate the discomfort and look anxiously out the windows. Kyle is stretchered into the ambulance, and Toni now covered with a foil blanket is ushered on board another ambulance that has just arrived. The ambulances leave followed by a patrol car.

A third police vehicle arrives, and three cops get out. The one that got out of the front passenger seat puts on a yellow braided flat cap and has a bar on his epaulettes. I guess that he is an Inspector or some equivalent and is in charge of this incident. Hard Nose approaches within intimate speaking distance with the senior cop and words are exchanged. Hard Nose calls over the fresh faced cop who jumps into the driver's seat. Hard Nose gets in the back with me and sits behind the driver. Before we leave I see the cops taking photographs and the fire crew about to do something with the plane.

CHAPTER 29

I languish in a police cell and lament how I got here. Self-pity could be an insistent foe and over the last seven hours had laid into me pretty good. The journey back to Isafjordur had been grim and interminable with hardly a word said; and with long periods where I felt as rough as a badger's arse. It was only made bearable by the handcuffs being moved to the front in a stacked position, which with one wrist on top of another made it impossible to straighten the arms. Still, it was a darn sight more comfortable than any rear position and I was grateful for it. Hard Nose had been unmoved, however Fresh Face had a nice streak and switched them round.

At the station I had been examined by a Police Doctor who documented my injuries. The Doctor declared that I was fit to be detained. My clothes were seized, and I was issued with a cheap grey sweatshirt, jogging bottoms and single use slippers. I was permitted a phone call. I called Annabel assuring her that I was fine and would get out of the mess that I had got myself into. I ended the call telling her I loved her - fearing I might not see her for a very long time.

Alongside the self-pity I dwell on my case, gathering the evidence to vindicate me and damn her. I line up the bullets I will fire to shoot her down in flames, then test for weaknesses in my defence. Gamekeeper and poacher are two faces of the same coin and I could flip from one to the other to suit. It is useful to do this to try and poke holes in your own case, to play the other side and to sabotage it with what ifs. If you can find those holes you can try to plug them and keep the case afloat. Though often a split was too wide to fix, or there were other leaks too. Then you had to stop bailing out the water and allow a sinking ship to sink.

The cell door opens and Gudjohnsen is there with a blue notebook tucked underneath his left arm. He is attired in a sharp, graphite grey suite and is sucking a sweet. I am somewhat glad to see him and that it made sense for him to be in on this.

"You look worse than the last time I saw you. Your face Mr. Cutter tells a story of woe," he comments drolly.

True without a doubt, though the humour if it is that from him, catches me off guard.

"Trials and tribulations Detective Gudjohnsen ... I'm wearing them."

He smiles half-heartedly and says,

"It is time for an interrogation. If you would like to follow me."

I nod and get up off the thin waterproof, anti-rip mattress that on top of the ten inch raise of concrete qualifies as a bed. I am led along a gloomy cell wing out through a set of key card secured doors, into a long carpeted corridor with a CCTV camera the other end. Along each side of the corridor there are pine coloured doors and Detective Gudjohnsen pushes and holds the third door on the right open. I step inside an interview room painted in a mellow green. There is a short, solid pine table with a spongy black top and two bolted down chairs either side. The table is pushed against the far wall and on it against the wall is a CD-ROM recording device. In the top corner of the opposite wall is a CCTV camera with a glowing red sensor. I take a seat facing the door like I'm supposed to, leaving the cop the ability to withdraw should the suspect become violent.

I hear a female voice in the corridor say something in Icelandic and Gudjohnsen continues to hold the door. A woman in a black suit with soft, white shirt underneath enters carrying a tray of coffees. She is slim to the point of thin and has chiselled cheek bones and bony hands. Her skin a translucent white and seemingly bloodless is complimented by stylishly severe auburn hair. It is difficult to tell how old she is, but I hazard a guess that she is in her mid-forties.

"Would you like a coffee Mr. Cutter, or may I call you Will?" she asks in flawless English.

"Yes, and yes," I reply.

I take a coffee from the tray and wrap my hands around the warmth. She picks up a notebook from the side of the chair next to the recorder and places it on the table. She takes a seat nearest to the machine and Gudjohnsen joins her on the adjacent seat.

"I am Detective Inspector Karlsdóttir and this as you know is Detective Gudjohnsen. In the next few seconds I will start the recording of this interview."

She presses the red record button and there is a five second beep as the seconds count forward on the blue digital display.

"This interview is being recorded at Isafjordur Police Station. The time is 16:39 hours on Tuesday 8th November 2017. I am interviewing ..." and she extends an open hand to prompt.

"William Jon Cutter born 12th of November 1971."

"Can you confirm that you are fit and well?" she continues.

"I've been a hell of a lot better. I was given GHB last night and you need to take a blood sample from me before it clears my system. But to answer your question I'm good to go."

"GHB?" she repeats in query.

"It is a sedative often used as a date rape drug."

"Okay, we'll have the Doctor see you again after the interview, but first I need to ask you again if you wish to have legal advice?"

"No, I'm just going to tell you everything so I don't need one. They are only of use if you plan to lie."

There is a flicker of amusement on Gudjohnsen's lips; then he says,

"You do understand the seriousness of the crimes which you have been detained for: homicide, causing danger to the public and causing substantial damage to property?"

"Of course."

"In this interview we will cover topics and the first topic I want to cover is you. Why have you come to Iceland?" Karlsdottir asks.

"Because my wife and I wanted to come here for a long time, and she died before we did. So ... so on the spur of the moment ... on a loose end I thought I'd go. Booked what I could get as soon as I could get it, and five days later I was on a plane to Keflavik."

"To do what?"

"The usual tourist stuff with some drinking thrown in."

The room is warm, and I am worn – frazzled and becoming flippant with it.

"You drink a lot?" she probes.

"A bit of late ... it helps take my mind off things."

"What kind of things?"

"Grief, uncertainty, frustration – the meat of life."

Gudjohnsen scribbles in his book and Karlsdottir poses another question.

"At present you are ill and not in work as a Police Sergeant is that correct?"

"I am off sick with stress," I reply with a tinge of embarrassment.

"You are suspended and under investigation for assaulting a suspect?"

I sit forward placing both palms on the table and looking her directly in the eye assert slowly,

"Not suspended – restricted and it was lawful use of force to effect an arrest. Did my Force mention the three commendations for bravery, or are you only worth the last piece of shit you were made to step in?"

"Would you describe yourself as a violent man?"

"Only when I need to be."

"When did you arrive and when were you due to return?"

"Last Tuesday and this Wednesday," and then I realize how she had just phrased return in the past tense.

"Let us talk about Antonia Brookes," says Karlsdottir.

"Good, I've a lot to say about her."

"How did you meet?"

"I met her at the Gaukurinn Bar in Reykjavik last Friday night. I was at the bar listening to a band when she came over to me. She started a conversation and bought me a drink. We talked and I bought her a drink in return. She seemed a little nervous and asked me to walk her back to her hotel. She said it was near to where I was staying."

"What hotel were you staying at?"

"The Storm."

"What hotel was Antonia staying at?"

I cant my head to the ceiling and open mouthed wait for the answer.

"The Leifur Eiriksson ... yeah. And if walking from the Gaukur-inn it is in the opposite direction to The Storm – nowhere near. That was her first lie."

"What happened next?"

"Well I've told Detective Gudjohnsen all this before."

"I want you to tell me," she says with effortless assertion.

"We get to an alley and she says she is good from here. We say our farewells and I remember that I have to text my daughter, so I stop to send a text. I hear a scream from the alley and go to investigate. I see Toni being attacked by two men. I decide to defend her and punch one of the men unconscious. I then get into a bit of a fight with the other guy and punch him uncon-scious too. We head back to my hotel and I ask her why the men had attacked her. She initially told me she didn't know why, but when I said I didn't believe her she came up with another story. Marcus her ex-partner and Adam his cousin were stalking her. Like I'm now supposed to be. So basically, she used me to deter Marcus and Adam from attacking her."

"What happened then?"

"She asked me to see her to her hotel and we caught a taxi. She invited me to her room, and we slept together. In the morning she said she was going on a trip around the Ring Road and I asked to go with her."

If you believed she was telling you lies why did you go with her?"

"It was exciting, she was exciting – I packed a bag and left my judgement at the hotel."

"Do you know why Antonia is in Iceland?"

"Now if you have found the gold then you'll believe me, if you haven't you won't."

I looked for a sign of acknowledgement and face is like a glacier, which indicated to me that they had found it.

"She came here to find Gorm's Gold ... Viking gold buried a thousand years ago; however, she didn't tell me this until I found her in Isafjordur. Up until then she said she was on a holiday like me."

"I don't want to get too far ahead. What happened on the trip?"

"Marcus and Adam run us off the road in a Land Rover Defender. They attacked us with baseball bats, snatched Toni and left me beaten on a ledge. There is a police report on it."

"Yes, I've read it."

"How do you think they found you?"

"Toni, I mean Antonia told me that Marcus had placed a tracking app on her phone. They were after the brooch."

"The brooch, what brooch?"

"The brooch Antonia had ... it is the key to locating the gold. Antonia's father Jim served in the United States Navy and for a few years was based at Keflavik. In his spare time Jim liked to explore the country and treasure hunt with a metal detector. This is how he met Jon Einarsson and became friends with him. Anyhow, on one of his trips he found this Viking brooch. The brooch remained just a brooch for over thirty years until Jon had an idea that it might be a key to finding Gorm's Gold. That is what she told me anyway."

"So how does the brooch work as a key?"

"The broach is a picture of two curling peaks with a cross made of amber. You look through the brooch and align the peaks, then the position of the cross tells you where the treasure is buried. Of course, you must know where these peaks are, and Jon did. The plan was that Toni would meet Jon in Isafjordur and together they would locate the gold."

"Okay we'll come back to that. We know that you left Borgarnes Police Station at 8pm on Saturday what did you do then?" asks Karlsdottir.

"Got the bus back to Reykjavik and slept at my hotel. Then the next morning I decided to look for her myself. I caught a plane from the city airport and flew to Isafjordur. I made some enquiries around town and identified that it was Jon Einarsson that I was after. The American lady at the café knew Jon well and told me where he lived. I went to the house and discovered that it had been broken into via the back door. I entered, searched the house and found Toni taped to a chair in the basement. Marcus, Adam and Marcus's new girlfriend Marta had stolen the brooch off Toni and kidnapped Jon. It was then that Toni told me about the brooch and Viking gold."

"Anything else happen at the house?" interjects Gudjohnsen, providing what I think is a cue to mention Adam. It could be a genuine unknowing question, a trap or a helping hand. One lie however could sour the whole pot.

"Adam came back with a knife in his hand. He was going to the basement to kill Toni and I confronted him on the stairs. He stabbed me in the shin, and I hit him with a spade ... he fell down the stairs. I then went outside, and this Marta was behind the wheel of a Mitsubishi Warrior. She saw me and drove off at speed."

"What happened to Adam?"

"He was able to get to the hospital."

Karlsdottir looks at Gudjohnsen and he makes a note.

"At that point you should have phoned the police; in fact, you should have phoned them as soon as you discovered that the house had been invaded ... don't you think?" says Karlsdottir leaving the point of the question lingering at my throat.

This was when I veered off track into unexplainable territory – a course of action I couldn't justify taking - the moment the Rubicon was crossed.

"Yes, I should have phoned the police."

"Then why didn't you Will?" the question pressing like a knife.

"I had a good life full of love and purpose and now it is an empty, sad mess. I am struggling, adrift, losing sight of the shore and she throws me a lifeline ... heh some lifeline more like a bag of bricks. Look I'm wrong. I can blame her for putting ideas into my head, but I agreed to go after the gold for self gain. I thought it would be a springboard to a new start, although truthfully it was not so much about the money, it was about her and the adventure."

"So, you did not inform the police because you both wanted to profit from finding the gold. And the involvement of the police would prevent that happening?" summarised Karlsdottir.

"Partly."

"The gold coins are of historic and cultural value and belong to the people of Iceland. It is a crime to find treasure and not notify the government ... to keep the treasure and sell for profit."

This confirmed that they had recovered the gold – they wouldn't be talking about a crime if they did not have evidence of one committed. I see an out – a way to wriggle off the hook.

"Yes, I figured that, however at that point I only agreed to help her find it. Smuggling it, selling it ... I did not commit to. There is always a reward for found treasure and in my mind that would be the best option."

Karlsdottir consults her notes.

"What happened next?"

"Toni had overheard where they were heading, and we took the Ford Ranger to go after them."

"Where were they heading?"

"South to Þingeyri, then west along the peninsula. The route is called ... Sva ... something. It is circular and goes past a light-house."

"Svalvogar?" offers Gudjohnsen.

"Yeah, that's the one. We drove along that route, along the coastline and just after ... there is a gap in the slope of the mountain which you can drive through. Their car was parked the other side. We stopped and climbed a sheep track onto the mountain. I used binoculars and saw Marcus, Marta and Jon hiking up the slope of a mountain with twin curling peaks. Toni and I flanked them," and I draw a curved line with my forefinger.

"Toni and I ambushed them and there was a standoff. Marcus struck Jon on the right side of his temple and knocked him out. He then held a spade over his head. I charged Marcus and put him down. There was a fight and Marcus and Marta got the worst of it and retreated. My face is evidence that it was a tough fight."

"Continue," encourages Karlsdottir.

"The brooch finds the spot and the metal detector pinpoints it. Toni and Jon dig and hit a big silver vase. I open the lid and it is full to the brim with shiny gold coins. We pull the vase out and count six hundred and twenty-four of these coins named Solidus of Irene. I mean I don't know what they are, but Jon does, and he is ecstatic. He starts saying that all the academics that doubted him would be proved wrong. He uses my phone to take pictures and gets me to video him explaining the discovery. Jon tells us that a government agency: one responsible for heritage and history would give a ten percent reward between the three of us. This works out to be a lot of money, one hundred and eighty thousand dollars of clean, legal money. I'm good with this and Antonia doesn't argue - so I think we are set to hand it over."

"Let me stop you a minute," says Karlsdottir.

"We have checked your phone and there are no pictures or videos of finding the gold."

"Antonia deleted them; I'll explain further on if I can."

Karlsdottir nods and I continue with my account.

"We load the gold coins onto the Ranger and head back to Isafjordur. On the way stop at the petrol station at Pingeyri to have some food and coffee. We order hot dogs and Jon tells us that he has a severe nut allergy, and he has almost died a couple times because of it. Antonia says she remembers her father talking about it. Jon then leaves us to go to the toilet, and immediately Toni complains that the reward money is going to be much lower and that she wants to take the coins - she wants real money for a new life. I tell her no and we quarrel. Jon comes back, then because Marcus had taken her phone Toni asks to use mine to phone her sick father. I ask Jon when he is going to inform the government of the find and he says first thing in the morning."

I finish the remains of my coffee and it has become tepid and barely drinkable from the time spent talking.

"We drive back to Jon's house, Toni tells me I'm right about the gold and I relax. We get in have some Black Death to drink and Toni goes upstairs to have a shower. Jon tells me some things about Toni's past that are different to what she told me, and I wonder what if anything she has told me is true. After her shower Toni comes down and says that she has run me a bath with salts. I go up and get in and Toni brings me a whisky from the bottle that is in my bag. I drink it, then in a moment of suspicion check the call log of my phone. I see the number that Toni had called earlier, and I put it into Google. The number belongs to K.B. Aviation: a small private charter company owned by pilot Kyle Banks. I phone the number and a guy answers and he must believe that I'm Toni because he calls me babe. He tells me the plane is being refuelled at Bildudalur, that he's hired a car, will be here in twenty minutes and is everything going according to plan."

"So, what did you think was going on?" asks Gudjohnsen shifting forward in the seat, his hands a steeple to his chin.

"That she was screwing Jon and I over and something bad was going to happen, which it did. I got out of the bath and felt light headed, which became much worse as I dried and dressed. The room was spinning, and I had to hold onto the wall to stand. I realized I had been drugged. I slid down the stairs and was all over the place. I'm in the hallway trying to get up when I see Jon at the living room door with his face all swollen and struggling to breathe. Toni sat him down and was talking to us. I can't remember much of what she said except her calmly saying I've put GHB in your drink Will. Then she pushed me over and kept Jon in the room until he died and kept me on the floor until I passed out," I recount, the last words loaded with rancour.

"So, are you saying that Antonia caused Jon Einarsson death?"

"Yes, I think she bought a bag of peanuts at the petrol station and knowing that he would go into Anaphylactic shock rubbed some on his glass. She pretended to help him, but she'd hidden his Epipens and phone; the lifelines that could have saved him. From there she just had to manage him as he grew weaker straining for breath, crawling along the floor, to die on his knees."

"Interesting," comments Karlsdottir, and in a reflective pause I see her compute what I have said with what they have found.

"Though you admit that you were drunk and drugged when this happened; your faculties very impaired."

"Yes, but I know what she did to Jon and what she then did to me."

"Then did to you. After this what did she do to you?"

"Kyle and Toni dragged me to a small wood above Isafjordur, hanged me by the neck from a tree and left me for dead. Toni then sent a suicide message to my children off my phone. I am woken by my daughter Annabel phoning me at half past four this morning."

"If you were hanged how did you survive?" queries Gudjohnsen.

"Luck ... the branch broke. I took pictures of the scene."

"Your phone is protected with a swipe code is it not? how was Toni able to access your phone when it is coded?" challenges Karlsdottir.

"Because when I gave Toni my phone at the petrol station I swiped it in front of her. She must have watched and remembered the swipe pattern."

"Explain what happened next?

"Getting out of the wood I saw that I was close to Jon's house, so I went back to see if he was alive. Toni and the gold had gone, and Jon was dead on the floor."

"How could you be sure, why didn't you phone for an ambulance, and again not notify the police?" prods Karlsdottir the glacier facade replaced with a hard edge of disapproval.

"I know dead when I see it; he was long gone. I know how this looks, but if I hadn't stopped them taking the gold I'd be in a worse position than I am in now. I would have a ropey story with no proof."

"So, you stole Jon Einarsson's Ford Ranger and drove to Bilduda-lur, where you used it to ram the plane off the runway almost killing the occupants?"

She has worked up a head of steam and I am getting it.

"I hit them at thirty miles per hour: enough to cancel the flight, not enough to kill them. Yes, I fully admit ramming the plane and I'd do it again to apprehend a murderer; lawful use of force Inspector to prevent escape."

"I think you forget that you are not a policeman here," is her riposte.

"You then drag the pilot from the plane and assault him isn't that true?"

"He tried to run. I prevented him from escaping too."

I am tiring from an already tired start. The warmth of the room is wilting, the toxic hangover brutal and unforgiving. Their questions and the effort of my answers wearing. All of them chisels, chipping away at what little there is left.

CHAPTER 30

"We've interviewed Antonia ..."

"Then you have a heap of lies to expose Inspector."

"She said she found the gold with Jon Einarsson and together they came up with the plan to fly it out of the country. Once they had got to the United States Jon was going to travel over and they would find a buyer for the coins. She agrees she met you at the Gaukurinn and after walking to your hotel, paid for a taxi to the Leifur Eiriksson where the two of you spent the night. In the morning she said you pressed to go on the road trip to Isafjordur with her, and reluctantly she agreed. During the journey to use her words, you *became creepy* and made her feel uncomfortable. She told you that she was going to drop you off at the next settlement. She then said you went crazy and grabbed the steering wheel causing the car to hit another vehicle and leave the road. According to her she was wearing a seatbelt and except for bruising her stomach she didn't get hurt, but you were not and banged your head badly against the dashboard knocking yourself out. Terrified she ran back to the road where a passing motorist picked her up. She phoned the police reporting the theft of the RAV4, then backed out because it would have been a distraction to finding the gold."

"Bravo ... but bullshit!"

The bullets so far are flying wide of the mark. She had taken what she couldn't avoid yet is evading everything else with a devious aplomb.

"What about Marcus and Adam?" I say feeling my anger being lit.

"She did not mention them, other than to say she told you at the Gaukurinn about her troubles with them back home," adds Gudjohnsen.

"Mr. Cutter I put it to you that you are infatuated with Antonia Brookes and you followed her to Isafjordur where using your policing skills you tracked Jon Einarsson down. You broke into his house, beat him and held him captive until he told you where Antonia was. You then suffocated him and stole his car. You faked your own hanging as well as police reports to cover your crimes of violence. If you confess now we can offer you a reduction in sentence."

My chest convulses with involuntary and muted laughter. I shake my head incredulous of what I had just heard and rush to pull it to pieces. It is a preposterous scenario and yet it fits, if you accept the premise of a man pushed to derangement by grief, stress and alcohol abuse. Could such a man, a man already predisposed to violence snap and go haywire – yes I suppose he could. If a man has lost the plot, then the plot no longer needed to make any sense.

"Mr. Cutter what do you say to that?" says Karlsdottir her tone sharpening.

"No, you are barking up the wrong tree Inspector. I'm the wrong man."

"No, we have the right man for some crimes, how many is the question?" Karlsdottir retorts.

And she is certainly a better adversary than Alexander Pritchard-Hayes.

Right, it is time to unload everything.

"Point one: speak to the waitress at the gas station diner at Pingeyri, she served three people: Jon, Toni and I at about 3:30 yesterday afternoon. Also speak to the cashier there because Toni bought chewing gum and I bet some type of nuts. And of course, there could be CCTV which will prove she is lying."

"Point two: the baseball bat and the cuts to my scalp. The handle of the bat that was seized will have my blood on it. It is evidence that there was a fight after the crash with Marcus and Adam."

"Point three: check the local hospitals for an American named Adam. He'll have a broken left arm and jaw. I caused those injuries at Jon's house and he stabbed me in the shin, unless you insist that I done that too."

"Point four: back triangulate the signal from my phone and it will show that I was in Svalvogar yesterday and travelled back to Isafjordur like I said."

"Point five: examine Kyle Banks's phone it will have my number in the call log. Called once by Toni and once by myself. If you believe Toni's story then there should be no call history between Kyle's phone and mine."

"Point six: get your pathologist to check for Anaphylaxis as a cause of Jon Einarsson's death."

"Point seven: Just ask yourselves who has the clear motive to kill Jon Einarsson: killing someone who I didn't know to find someone who I barely know or killing someone and attempting to kill another who stood in the way of five and a half million dollars ... think on it detectives."

CHAPTER 31

The interview had concluded shortly after issuing them the investigative plan. The way I had laid it out to them had bordered on impudence. Even so, in the summation of things it didn't matter, with my liberty in the balance it was not a time to pussy-foot around, and I cared not whether I offended or pleased. Before being returned to the cell a Doctor had taken a blood sample and I was permitted another phone call. I tried to contact Nathan, however he must have been on an exercise because his phone went straight to voicemail. I leave a message, which delivered off the cuff became awkward and rambling.

Back in the cell I sleep a little but not much. I drink often trying to flush out the toxins and in between bouts of staring at the ceiling pace the cell. The minutes stretch out and the hours seem stuck. For supper I am given a bowl of lamb cowl with a bread roll, which for jail food isn't bad. I pace up and down the cell racking up steps that a now dead Fitbit can't count. Although I am listless I keep doing circuits of the cell hoping to drive myself to an undeniable sleep.

In a permanently half lit cell time becomes imperceptible. I envisage solitary confinement with time shapeless and indistinct, as subordinate only to loneliness in the tally of its deprivations. I lay down underneath the blanket and as a diversion think back to the championship bouts I fought. I was good, but not quite good enough to earn a title beyond my backyard. I came within an inch, though in a way it would have been kinder if it were a mile - because I had replayed and replayed that sliver of an error, that hook that had almost salvaged a triumph from the deep maw of defeat - deeper still for three years straight. I drift off with thoughts of past glories and just as many of what could have been.

I wake sometime during the night or early morning. It is dark outside, so it is one of the two - and I hope it is the latter. They can keep me in custody for twenty-four hours, after which time I must be taken to a judge who will decide whether I am detained or released. A jailer brings a pot of microwaveable porridge that tastes of cardboard, and a small, weak coffee in a Styrofoam cup. I force both down and get back to lapping the cell clockwise, anti-clockwise and figure of eight to mix it up. My shin hurts a lot less than it did, and I even feel up to short spurts of light shadow boxing.

I am rolling at the waist into a hook when I hear the clack of the hatch dropping on the cell door.

"If you have finished punching people imaginary or otherwise I need to speak with you," says Gudjohnsen, his shadowed face only partially visible through the hatch.

"You have a captive audience Detective Gudjohnsen, go ahead."

"Not here, come with me," and perhaps it is imagined but I swear I detect a warming in his voice.

I follow Gudjohnsen out of the cell complex and into a small, blue painted office with colour coordinated seats. There is a whiteboard on the far wall and alongside it what I think is a full length calendar. Underneath this a wooden book case: its books interspersed with potted cacti and ceremonial photographs of a policeman receiving honours that aren't Gudjohnsen. Gudjohnsen sits behind a flat pack desk. He pushes the keyboard and monitor to one side so that we can clearly see each other. I notice in proper mugs two steaming coffees and a plate of Danish pastries. He invites me to sit. I grab the end seat against the wall and drag it nearer the desk.

Gudjohnsen is wearing the same suit as yesterday and has the pallor and sagging eyelids of a man that has worked straight through the night.

"Help yourself," he says.

And still hungry after a paltry breakfast I select a custard Danish from the plate and get right into it. Something is afoot but I wait for him to explain. The coffee is good, and the Icelandic Danish is sublime, so I am in no rush to start talking. Gudjohnsen puts a half-finished pastry down as I am picking up my second. He wipes his mouth and says,

"We have made significant progress in the case and we are no longer treating you as a suspect in the murder of Jon Einarsson. If you fully cooperate as a prosecuting witness you will face no charges. It means you will have to provide testimony in a criminal trial."

"Yes, I understand, and I will," I reply without a moment's hesitation and huge sense of relief.

"What has happened since our interview?" I ask, curious as to what had changed.

Gudjohnsen smiles, loosens his shirt collar and relaxes into the chair.

"One story gained support, and another fell apart. We found footprints in the house: some were from your Altberg boots, and a couple belonged to the Harkila Trail boots worn by Kyle Banks. The left boot even had the same indent from the sole where a chunk of the grip is missing. We also found several pine needles along the side of both boots. Phone work connected your phones and triangulation off phone masts put Kyle in the Isafjordur area on Monday night. It didn't take much to break Kyle. He was sweating rocks before we began the interview, and when we hit him with a few facts ... he folded like a bad hand of cards."

There is now a satisfied smile raising normally straight set lips, and he seems altogether less uptight.

"Kyle's lawyer asked for a deal: a plea bargain offering admission to theft of valuables and obstruction of justice for misrepresenting your murder as suicide. Kyle is providing full cooperation for a reduced sentence. He has told us Antonia approached him around six months ago at a bar and grill outside Albany airport called J.T. Maxies. She told him she worked in sales for a pharmaceutical company and travelled a lot. They began seeing each other and as he describes - things got serious quick. Four months in she confides in him about the gold and recruits him to fly it back to the States in return for a half share. Even though he suspected he was being used he didn't care - he was too far in and would take her however he could get her - do pretty much whatever she asked. Kyle had quite a journey. He flew his little Cessna from Albany to Portsmouth, New Hampshire, and from there over the border to Quebec City. He then headed to Iqaluit in the eastern province of Nunavut before flying onto Nuuk in Greenland and eventually to Bildudalur ... where you smashed his plane into the sea."

Gudjohnsen pauses, his hands forming a low steeple above his chest and awaits a reaction he doesn't receive.

"We looked at the bigger picture Will; do you play chess?"

"Badly, yeah."

"Well if this is chess: Banks is merely a pawn, and you a knight. Both pieces to be sacrificed to reach the end game ... which is the capture of the king."

"Toni!" I chime in, playing along with a fitting analogy.

Gudjohnsen nods and leans to the table to pick up his coffee.

"What have you agreed on?" I ask.

"Six years and with his testimony she will go away for twenty. We considered pushing for attempted murder, however he maintains that he thought you were dead already, which is plausible ... this way both of them will get punished."

I slowly and subtly nod – it was the right call leading to the right outcome.

"You have a strong case against her?"

"We didn't at first, but now we do, and it is getting stronger the more we find out about her. We have been speaking with New York State Police who have been most helpful. For instance, in

2008 she was tried but acquitted of embezzling large quantities of drugs from the hospital where she worked. In the summer of 2013, her husband Brandon Zingano was found dead in his hot tub: the cause of death accidental drowning due to drug and alcohol consumption. The Coroner's report lists alcohol, cannabis and a moderate amount of Oxycodone - a prescription opioid commonly and illegally misused as being in his system at the time of death. Antonia Zingano as she was then had frolicked in the hot tub with her husband that fateful night. According to the report she went to bed leaving Brandon drinking and listening to music."

I listen transfixed, my mind racing ahead to join the dots. I conjure a scene with a steamy, bubbling hot tub and a tattooed Brandon with his arms over the rim dozing into his shoulder. Empty bottles of beer on the apron of the tub. One down to the dregs laced with GHB. Toni sitting the other side patiently waiting for the deepness of sleep. When certain she edges around and carefully lowers an arm into the water. Brandon starts to sink into the water and Toni manipulates the motion, steadying the head to partially submerge it, causing restful, accidental death – fuck! she is a piece of work.

"Lightning has struck twice would you agree. Antonia inherited a tattoo shop, a house and twenty thousand dollars from a savings account. Zingano's family were unhappy with the circumstances of his death and called for a review. There was no basis to re-open the case and it was shelved. Antonia had some trouble with the family so sold the shop on and moved to North Tonawanda. From what I know now I think she got away with murder," says Gudjohnsen shrugging his eyebrows.

Her words come back to me "Our relationship cooled ... and I felt it was time to go it alone" - a casual lie or a gross euphemism for what she had done.

"We have her buying chewing gum, hot chocolate and two peanut butter and chocolate bars at the gas station. It seems she left an impression on the cashier who remembers her clearly. The autopsy shows that Jon ingested peanut butter and chocolate, and that Anaphylaxis is a probable cause of death. A mug was found in the kitchen containing traces of chocolate. We are working on the assumption that she melted the bars in the microwave and mixed it in with the hot chocolate. We assigned a detective to build a picture of Jon Einarsson. He was a local character, a well liked man and by all accounts dedicated to discovering and preserving Icelandic heritage. Several local historians will attest to Jon's ambition to find Gorm Thorsen's gold for the people of Iceland. And for his place in history as the man who found it."

"What about Marcus, Adam and Marta?" I ask half wishing I hadn't.

"Ah! Marcus Rocher, Adam Kucera and Marta Rodriguez."

"Kyle doesn't know anything about them, didn't know anything about you until the last hour and Antonia denies their involvement. We know that Kucera discharged himself from Isafjordur Medical Centre on Monday evening. We are checking the passenger manifest with the airport this morning. We have now placed markers on them and if they try to fly out of the country at Akureyri or Keflavik, they will be stopped and arrested."

"So, I am I free to go?"

"Yes, after you sign my statements," he says half-jokingly, displaying an edged smile.

CHAPTER 32

It is late as the police car pulls up outside the Storm Hotel. I ease out the passenger side and thank the driver Ari for the lift. It had been a long drive and one which I am sorry the affable, young cop would now have to repeat. Gudjohnsen was keen that I did not wander and come to more grief, so had me delivered to the door.

I enter the hotel and slalom through a huddle of tourists going the other way. I hear snippets of their idle conversation and feel a world away. I get to a room that by now I should be familiar with and yet is still a novelty. I kick off the custody slops and linger in a hot shower. I turn my face into the jets wanting the powerful streams to blast clean, to blast it all away. I wonder at the countless people that had tried to scrub the dirt from their souls - vainly scouring their skin of an internal sin.

Clean but not cleansed I dry off and go to bed. The room clock ticks and regret nags. I had done little wrong and put what I had right. It had worked out, nonetheless there is a ring of defeat to the whole saga. I had come through the fire, although not without getting burnt - betrayal burns like a red hot poker through the heart.

I hit breakfast like a starved man then go and get the case from the room. I hand the key over to the receptionist and see a computer monitor displaying a news story. On the screen is a photograph of the Cessna being winched out of the water. I hadn't given thought to the impact the story would have and the coverage it would generate. I roll the thought around my head for a minute. Iceland had a tiny population and one of the lowest crime rates in the world – it would headline for days.

I wait in the foyer for the bus to the airport. It is unpleasantly cold outside, and my coat and gloves are in an evidence room in Isafjordur. I am wearing a grey Berghaus fleece that is roomy enough to accommodate underneath a thick woollen jumper and long-sleeved thermal top. Blue jeans and grey Sketchers complete a casual outfit. After a restless twenty minutes the bus arrives, and I am on my way home - home to a career in tatters and a place in the unemployment line. This fiasco would nail the coffin lid shut and drop a ton of soil over the top. The Job hated reputational harm or bringing discredit to the police service as it is officially titled in the Code of Conduct. Being mixed up in murder, theft and an assortment of other offences more than met the definition.

The bus docks at a bay and I shuffle out with the other passengers. I collect my case and carry it towards a grubby grey terminal with a front of outward angled glass. Some passengers push baggage trolleys, while mostly the young travel light. I see a female Tui Rep in a cyan soft-shell jacket herding a party of fresh tourists to a waiting coach. I manoeuvre around them and come face to face with Marcus Rocher.

Marcus sitting against a concrete security bollard has an unlit cigarette poised on his lips. The top lip appearing neatly cut like it had been snipped by a scissors, and not by my crude left fist. He looks up at me through his brow, his right arm in a sling, the left hand torching the tip of the cigarette. Adam Kucera is standing next to him facing away; puffs of smoke dispersing around him. Marta is knelt behind Marcus attaching a label to a holdall.

I drop my case – round fucking four. Marcus straightens up. The expression on his face akin to the wary curiosity of an alerted fox.

"Ad," he says in warning.

Adam turns as slowly as a rusted tap. The movement is painful and laboured and punctuated with grunts. The left arm below the elbow is in a cast and the right hand holds a four toed cane. The left side of the jaw is bloated and a palette of dark purple and emerging jaundice. I've had my fill of fighting. Showing my palms, I say,

"No trouble; I want to talk."

"Jump in front of a bus you cunt!" mutters Adam through the right side of a wired mouth.

"Not to you. You're only good for smacking around and I'm bored of that. I want to talk to you Marcus."

Marcus's eyes search about and beyond me.

"She's fucked you off hasn't she?" and a satisfied smirk occupies his lips - a prophecy coming to pass.

I ignored my intuition and deserved a chorus of I told you so's.

"If it were only that," I lament on the tragic coupling of treachery and folly.

"Oh! she screwed you over good did she? Well I did tell you didn't I, you dumb fuck."

The words a blend of three quarters spite with a smattering of sympathy.

"Yes, you did, albeit at the time you were preparing to take my head off with a bat. Look two minutes and we are out of each other's lives."

"Don't trust him Marcus," urges Marta.

"It's all right Marta, if he had wanted to he could have finished me on the mountain. Besides I have a couple of questions of my own. Fire away fella."

"Who is she?" I ask wanting to get to the bare bones.

Marcus takes a moment to consider, as if it is unknowing and can't be compiled. Then switching between being spiteful and wistful, and sometimes a hybrid of the two takes a stab at describing Antoni Brookes.

"What can I tell you that you probably haven't figured out already? She is a wonderful liar, an ace manipulator of men and occasional women if it suits. A talented tattooist, hot as hell and destructive as an Oklahoma twister. Man, that woman is dangerous in a fight. And afterwards when you think it is over - I wasn't kidding about sleeping with one eye open. I got scalded when I didn't and got my shoulder broke when I did. Loves to party, snorting lines, popping pills; she sells a hell of a lot of them from the shop too. Got a thing going with a bunch of crooked Doctors where she gets fake prescriptions. She likes to steal for the fun of it. Spontaneous shit like lifting a wallet off a bar table or pocketing a tip left for a waitress. Makes a habit of defrauding insurance companies and gets a buzz from gambling and adrenaline sports like me. That's Toni and I don't know all of it."

My face must have communicated something he enjoyed because he continued to piss over an already wet parade – shit talking is evidently in his blood.

"I rode that lightning bolt for two years and what ... she left you broke and broken hearted in four days! What did she do ... what did she do to you bud?"

Marcus looks like a salivating dog already savouring the treat he is going to get. I decide not to give to it him. I know, and what I don't I can assume – and assume the worst. I give a peeved smile and say,

"Something she is going to pay twenty years for. So long Marcus have a good trip."

I pick up my case and pass them with sneers and curses on their lips.

CHAPTER 33

11:04am Monday 28th November 2017.

The sand shifts from beneath my feet as I scramble up the dune. Running up the side and over the crest on a track hedged by needle point grass. My lungs working like bellows operating at the edge of capacity. Then down in splashing leaps and bounds desperately repaying a debt of oxygen owed. Back up another, trainers scooping sand and shelves of it falling away. Momentum stolen by the cold, damp sand slipping me to a moving stop. I dig my hands into the grassy sand and fight my way up the stubborn giant. At its crown, thighs burn, and lungs burst bloody as I lope forward in a lightheaded delirium. From here the ground undulates over the back of smaller dunes, and I am able to recover and branch off on the many forks and circuits.

The first run back is the hardest and feels like a punishment a Drill Sergeant would dish out to a failing recruit. I slice a line up a low dune and run its narrow brow glimpsing the estuary to the River Neath where I will turn back. At a fork I pick a track that leads me inward past a fish bait farm and the old BP site. The plant long levelled to concrete slab and rusting perimeter fence. I plod on, the needle grass piercing my legs through the tight black leggings and leaving wet licks. The light breeze salty, but with an element of something the nearby paper mill is adding to the air.

Continuing to a basin of open sand freckled with iron ore and rutted by off road motorbikes. I flit a long diagonal line over the final dune skipping and scrabbling over the tumps to the final stretch. My feet sink deep in crusty sand as I jog past driftwood and the detritus of industry: a tangle of frayed rope, a broken bucket, and empty tub of paint, a lonely shoe. The last yards to the blue metal lamp post; one of several sentinels lining the banks of the estuary guiding the cargo ships to the Briton Ferry Dock.

I look across to Jersey Marine and a vacant shore. The M4 motorway and Briton Ferry bridge to my right, a grey, unsettled sea to my left with a tanker on the horizon, and behind the long expanse of Aberavon Beach. Beyond it the immense cranes of the steel works; three titans bearing the load of a town. The theme of *Knight Rider* plays from the phone holder velcroed to my bicep – I couldn't listen to *Get Carter* any longer without a flood of unhealthy emotion. If I had felt fitter I would have ignored it and carried on running. Instead I answer on the fifth ring.

"Hello," I manage to get out.

"Will is that you?" the voice familiar though not enough to recognize who it belonged to.

"Yes," I reply keeping the answers necessarily brief.

"It's Pete Drummond; how are you doing?"

"Oh … hi Super, I'm feeling better, I think I'm finally turning a corner."

Pete Drummond is a Superintendent and an old colleague of mine. He had been my Inspector for a couple of years, and we had got on – he had time for thief takers and no time for scrotes. In the last five years he had really knuckled down, played the game and climbed two ranks. But he wasn't one of those Corporate Cats – at least he hadn't been. He had a rugby player's mentality, forged on the field, the bar and the tour bus. Pete could rub shoulders with high and low alike – I just hope he hadn't lost it going up the ladder.

"I've some good news for you Will. The Larkin complaint's

been dealt with. I've wrote it off and the I.P.O.C. agrees with me. It should have never got this far, ought to have been put to bed months ago."

I suddenly feel relieved of a weight I'd been carrying. Like someone had taken the load and thrown it into the wind.

"So how long have you been on P.S.D.?" I ask.

"Nearly two months. I've been reviewing all the cases and this one should have been binned as soon as Larkin got potted on the assault police charge. I've got some views on this type of thing, which I think you know. Larkin is a thug, and if you live by the sword then you can't complain when you get cut."

Drummond hadn't changed.

"I couldn't agree more, thank you for putting it right."

"We got to hear about your escapades in Iceland," and my heart plunges.

"I've been forwarded an email from a Detective Superintendent Hermannsson. It is most complimentary; seems you foiled an International plot to smuggle stolen Viking gold out of the country. That is not a sentence I have said often," he jokes.

It informs us that you are required to return to Iceland in May to give evidence in the trial. You're hell of a boy Will, you haven't changed have you?"

And I imagine him on the other side of the phone shaking his head.

"No unfortunately for me I haven't."

"One more piece of good news: the transfer is back on and I've pulled some strings. It isn't official so keep it under your hat, but it is looking good for Team 2 Response Port Talbot. I've had a chat with Glyn Jones the Super of Western Operations, and they've got a Sergeant's vacancy there they need to fill. I've put in a good word. Now get back to work because they won't transfer you sick."

"Yes, boss I will; thanks again," and a smile came like a great big rip across my face.

Port Talbot, Port Tablet, Port Toilet – San Portablo as the crews I had worked with called it. I could be coming home to my dirty steel town of spit and venom. A town of shame and glory, upbringing and belonging. You've found your way back, are no longer lost, when you come home.

19322456R00129

Printed in Great Britain
by Amazon